GRAMMATICAL DREAMS

MURRAY POMERANCE

Grammatical Dreams

GREEN INTEGER
KØBENHAVN & LOS ANGELES
2020

GREEN INTEGER
Edited by Per Bregne
København / Los Angeles
(323) 937-3783 / www.greeninteger.com

Distributed in the United States by
Consortium Book Sales & Distribution / Ingram Books
(800) 283-3572 / www.cbsd.com

First Green Integer Edition 2020
Copyright ©2020 by Murray Pomerance
Back cover copy ©2020 by Green Integer
All rights reserved.

Cover: Photograph of Murray Pomerance
Book Design: Pablo Capra

LIBRARY OF CONGRESS CATALOGING-IN-PUBLICATION DATA
Pomerance, Murray [1946-]
Grammatical Dreams
p. cm — Green Integer: 211
ISBN: 978-1-933382-34-0
i. Title. ii. Series. iii. Translator

Green Integer books are published for Douglas Messerli
Printed in the United States of America

CONTENTS

being a most merry and pleasant historie,
not unprofitable for
citizens, farmers, and all sorts of laborers,
nor in any way harmful,
very fit to pass away the tedium
of long evenings.

Sometimes a thousand twangling instruments
Will hum about mine ears; and sometime voices

The Tempest, III.ii.135-36

Grammatical Dreams

SHE HAD A SMOCK,

did she not? The smock was silk. Having scraped the pine gum off his naugahyde with a fork, she carefully sat. We had roasted chestnuts in the heat of August, she and I. We had strolled. I had been the hysterical one, oh yes. The downpour came suddenly upon us. The bus was covered inside with soot and smelled throughout of gasoline. We were suddenly hiding in a labyrinth of lilacs. Her smock, silk, was brightly colored with an orange print. I loved that smock. "Who was that woman, the lady with the two plump children . . . ?" she said quite coldly. Nothing at all more: "Who was that woman, the lady with the two plump children . . . ?" And then, inconsequentially, and it was still raining, "My brother has to pay adult fare because he is twelve." We had roasted chestnuts. We strolled. "Where, on all buses, on every bus?" said I, but she didn't answer, "Where does he have to pay? Where?" Her brother, now appearing, wore a sky-blue kerchief, of all places around his wrist, smoked a cigarette, odd for someone so young. Odd in some places. He waved it at me, as a French movie star would, and he had to pay adult fare. "Because he's twelve," I told myself, and oddly, "Photosynthesis' is exclusively a plant function." Slowly she sipped a glass of warmed milk which her mother had prepared for her. Seven black crows.

SCHMALLING WAS AGONIZED

on Saturday nights, this was a Saturday night, or maybe, so computer dating services looked marvelous. But instinctively he knew—did he not?—they were not his cup of tea. "The politics of sex never changes," he told himself self-congratulatorily, looking in the mirror which was tarnished and a little warped and yellowing and which had lost some of its capacity to reflect what we most wanted to see. We had roasted chestnuts. You. I gave serious consideration to Schmalling's words, etching them upon a delicate screen of the slowly opening, tolling chrysanthemums. My brother has to pay an adult fare because he is twelve. He looked into the mirror which was tarnished. My brother has to pay. The light of the dawn softened the profile of the tor. A blue balloon went up. Great herons feed slowly and fly high. Feed and fly. And fly and fly. Feed and fly and fly. Once-distant thunder now booming very loudly, the tempest broke around us. We could not make arrangements. Schmalling was agonized, I tell you. We stood and listened. He said in an agony, "I haven't read *Ulysses*, can you believe that?" It was in my hand, heavy. The muscles of my palm. He was white with agony. The downpour came upon us. The vitrine we examined was overfull of reticles and spectacles. "Everyone I know has read it," he said, "but I have not cracked the cover." Then Schmalling explained that he did not really believe everyone had read it, but that he had this strange fear, whenever he met anyone, and instantly, that they had read it, and he believed utterly that they had read it, and so everyone Schmalling met became, instantly, someone who was superior because he had read *Ulysses*. The palm of my hand. My brother has to pay an adult fare because he is twelve; he has a little silky fawn's hair on his forearms. On the far lawn old Spot lies around all day. "I haven't read *Ulysses*, at my age, can you imagine?" said Schmalling. My brother has a little silky fawn's hair. Spot lies on the lawn. The tempest broke. You. You.

THE WIND

disbursed the seeds. The wind dispersed the seeds. Both. Schmalling, who hadn't read much, so he said, always wore blue, never red. "Not much. Don't read. I don't." Not read, not red. My brother had hair, and there was a hare. The hare stood upon the lawn, near Spot, who lay with his veal bone. The tempest broke. The wind disbursed the seeds and dispersed the seeds. Schmalling danced and Schmalling sang. Hey nonny. An old man. We stood, let me tell you, by the high castle, near the wind-whipped dune grass, in the snow, by the gray sea, as night fell, and the beach was flat, the sand glassine, and as we walked I saw a light in the castle. Was it her? We climbed the rocks and scaled the wall, we climbed the rocks and scaled the wall, up, up the wall, and in the window was a candle and she was brushing her hair. The tempest broke. Across the beach, running, was it her?

I TRAVELED

thirteen hours by air. My brother has to pay an adult fare because he is twelve. I carry his bags for him. I carried them. My palm. His chin was between his thumb and forefinger. He had green bags. He had brown bags. Nobody knew. Nobody knew and no one cared that he had lost, somehow in a public lavatory, his favorite drawing of the Tower of Pisa. Somebody is lying to cover up his own guilt. The winters of my childhood were long.

"I'M TREATING THE COW

for a kidney disease," said La Porte, the veterinarian. "Climb higher," said La Perla, the mountaineer. "You need to cut down on carbohydrates," said Laperra, the dietitian, the advisor. Dietetic advisor, giving advice to clinicians who became dieticians. "Your right arm must come over your head," said Leppard, the swimming instructor, "all the way, all the way over, yes over, like this, yes like this, over." Diamond lights in the cut glass of the vase with the mauve roses. "This is an ore and this is a pyrite," said Penucho, the geologist. "The truck driver died as the result of an accident," said Lambrade, the coroner. "We should play this section half as quickly," said Lapsou, the conductor, "Don't worry about it." "My suggestion is that the building should face south," said Pestrel, the architect. "Your ticket expired last month," said Laidlaw, the fare collector. "Which corner do you want, this corner or that corner?" said Lee, the taxi driver. "Do two and two always equal four?" asked Levine, the psychologist. "Your right arm must come over your head, a nice round arc, all the way, nice," said the swimming instructor. "There are fewer spots on the sun this year than last year," said Parker-Peley, the astronomer. "Your business is making a very small profit," said Pastoureau, the accountant. "Your right arm must come over your head," said the swimming instructor. "I need mortar," said Peters, the bricklayer. "I shall have the tiger ready for you next month," said Lasseter, the taxidermist. "The disease is bacterial," said Lexeter, the pathologist. "If you sue, you will surely not win," said Ling, the barrister. "Cut, print, wrap," said Lupu, the film director. "I adore pistachios," said Pemberton, the waitress. "Never plant tropicals next to alpines," said De Vallières, the garden designer from Asnières. "The Lord cherish and keep you," said Poe, the minister. "Your right arm must come over your head," said the swimming instructor. "I adore pistachios," said the waitress. "There are fewer spots on the sun this year than last year," said the astronomer. "I adore pistachios," said the waitress. "There are fewer spots on the sun this year than last year," said the astronomer. "Your right arm must come over your head," said the swimming instructor, "like a mountain." "Your business is making a very small profit," said the accountant. "Your ticket expired last month," said the fare collector. "Climb higher," said the mountaineer. "I adore pistachios," said the waitress. "You need to cut down on carbohydrates," said the dietitian. "Your right arm must come over your head," said the swimming instructor. "Do two and two always equal four?" asked the psychologist. "We should play this section half as quickly," said the conductor, "And you shouldn't worry. Just play. Just play." "Your right arm must come over your head," said the swimming instructor. "Do two and two always equal four?" asked the psychologist. "We should play this section half as quickly," said the conductor. "You need to cut down on carbohydrates," said the dietitian. "Do two and two always equal four?" asked the psychologist. "We should play this section half as quickly," said the conductor. "You need to cut down on carbohydrates," said the dietitian. "We should play this section half as quickly," said the conductor. "You need to cut down on carbohydrates," said the dietitian. Your right arm must come over your head. The disease is bacterial. We should play this section half as quickly. Do two and two always equal four?

AS FOR CHURCH,

we found there the _____. We had been
hunting for what one would find, this much was
true, the ambulance and its crew, and the light was
beautiful, but there was a queer space both enclos-
ing and separating us and as we looked up the experience came to a hinge. Leaves drooped off in every
direction. I had a pencil but it lost its point. The
notification was very clearly inscribed, and following it we went to the church and found there the
brutal _____.

TAKE

a moment. Take, take a moment or else a moment. The moment was huge. Take a breath, he took a breath, she will take a breath, they had taken a breath, we would have taken breath but we could not break bread. They could not imagine having been capable of taking a breath. Were you to consider taking a breath it would be a breath, it would breathe, it would take, it would, were you to. Taken, a breath taken. Take a moment or else a moment, take a moment that is huge. The previous life.

SEVEN

black crows. The men. His uncle. You. The children. The ambulance and its crew. An old man. An old man. You. An old man. The children. An old man. The men. The men. The men. The men. The ambulance and its crew. The men. An old man. The children. His uncle. The men. The men. His uncle stood. The men ran out. The ambulance and its crew arrived, left, waited, worked, interrupted, disrupted, displaced, replaced, reacted, rejoiced. His uncle. His underwater exploration. His uncle the underwriter. The ambulance and its crew. You. You spent. You reacted. You reported. You repotted. You spotted and repotted. You could not. You could not but. You could hardly. You could even. You could have. If you could have. His uncle the underwriter. The ambulance and its crew. The men. You could have. If only you could have. The men. The men running. You could have. The men reacting. You could have thought. You could have tonight. You could not have thought. The men. You could not have. You could never have. Tight, the ambulance and its crew. You could never have.

The children. Splashing, the children displacing. The ambulance and its crew. You could never have wanted to. You could always. We could. You could. The men. The men. An old man. An old, old man. Seven black crows.

ANOREXIA

nervosa is a condition in which a person starves herself and loses an excessive amount of weight. Herself, himself; herself, himself. Parking is an impossibility. Agility, impossibility. The feelings of the hostess were hurt. Dirt, hurt, dirt, dirt, hurt, hurt. So you have a hammer? Speaking personally, I do not sweat. I, you, I, you. You can't truly enjoy a sport unless you know the basic rules. Can, can't. Can, can't. Can, can't. Rules. But with cricket, rules are little or nothing. I say, with cricket. Someone from the verger's is always assiduously inscribing the score in a black book, with a sharpened pencil. Scoring, snoring. Scoring, snoring. Snoring, scoring. Snoring, scoring. I say, with cricket. The Math Department is offering a seminar for English teachers on formulas so they will recognize formulaic writing. Teachers of English, teachers who are English. I say, the Math Department. The Four Horsemen of the Apocalypse are Conquest, Slaughter, Famine, and Death. I traveled thirteen hours by air. Parking an impossibility, the feelings of the hostess hurt, we picked up a hammer. My brother has to pay an adult fare because he is twelve.

SOMEONE FROM THE VERGER'S

is always inscribing. Schmalling stood up slowly.
The weird little man eating soup at the round table
is lovable, hat and all. One felt doubly mortified.
The weird little man eating soup at the round table
is lovable, hat and all. Schmalling stood up slowly.
He doesn't want no trouble, he wants adventure.
Schmalling stood up slowly. One felt singularly (singularly) mortified. My brother has no choice but to
pay an adult fare. My brother pays. Schmalling stood
up slowly. Men in red (red) collars make themselves
noticeable at the perimeters. Parking is an impossibility. He doesn't want no trouble. (No trouble isn't
what he wants.) You can't always get what you want.
Seven black crows. Get, not get. They sat together
and enjoyed the warm glow (the poppies, the plaster
casts, the Irish setters). The weird little man is lovable enough (lovable enough, not lovable), hat and
all. One felt singularly mortified. One felt singularly. One felt, two felt. Singularly, doubly, to a crisis or
a confusion. Crisis, confusion. Schmalling stood up.
My brother. Men in red. Adventure. You can't get.
Lovable enough, not lovable.

AT THE BACK

of the church, inscribed in a stained glass, if we had looked we would have found the true facts. We looked up into the apse, however, and our thoughts came to a hinge. We looked up into the apse. We looked up into the apse, however, and our hearts were together, we looked up into the apse. The choirboys sang Bach, a little happily. Bach, a little happily. Bach. The choirboys sang Bach. Bach, a little happily. The choirboys sang Bach. The choirboys sang Bach. The choirboys looked up into the apse. Then we cast our eyes around and saw that all the place was lit with a green light. And we had a pocket flash but no batteries.

PIG

pog peg. The man said, "Pig pog peg." The man raised his hand sternly into the air and said, "Pig pog pig pog peg." [Shifting uncomfortably in one's seat] Pen pun pug pog [Perusing] pig fig fog fig [Perusing and calculating] fig fog pog fog pog pig peg log dog dig dog [Beginning an estimation, stirring a lump of sugar into the demitasse] log dog dig dog log leg log lox box fox fix fig pig pig pig fig wig whig big jig big jig jog log pog [Clearing the throat, taking a little marzipan, turning on a lamp] frog flog floor door doom room roof aloof aloud crowd crown down drain pain rain stain shine mine thine fine twine line pine [Recalibrating, opening the notebook, making a telephone call, debating the merits, deciding against, expressing a sentiment, voting no, closing the book, walking out, declining to take telephone calls] tine tined two-tined three-tined wined spined Stein Stein Stein Stein Stein Stein Stein Stein [Filling in the chit, waiting in the huge blue room under the dome, offering small talk, working at the baize-covered ancient table from Les Baux] wine dine dire sire shire shift rift shine spine fine dine dine spine dine spine dine shire sire spire sire shire shire spire [Calling the agent in Old Tucson, booking the ticket, reading the pamphlet, doing up the seat belt, checking the baggage tag, finding the limousine, scanning the countryside, Chantilly, counting cows, counting cows, counting cows] tires fires fares where there stare lair ne'er spare prayer player planner spanner spastic plastic fancy yacy stoulie strombouli pastafazooli yuley yule rule fool drool yule rule fool drool cool drole stole role pole knoll stroll whole sole spasm plasm ectoplasm [Stubbing it out] protoplasm neologism interactionism [The cigarette] miasmoplasm [Waiting for the filling of the prescription] redundoplasm mitochondryoplasm ferracetoplasm [Stubbing out the cigarette] mesoplasm endoplasm riboplasm ribonucleoplasm ribonucleotide ribosome [Smelling the corridor, the cleaning fluid like Chartreuse, the yellow bricks, the blackboards, the ancient rows of seats where the initials L.O.R.V. are carved again and again, carved, carved again, Chartres] rye bread ribase acetase ketase Swiss on rye aldase streptase striptease streptose lactose fructose grandiose grandly handily hungrily [Filing complaint, issuing complaint, voicing complaint, twisting to get comfortable in one's seat] stunningly winningly winning spinning beginning [Perusing the windows of Fauchon and of Maître Vou and of Andy's Hardware, Scranton, Pennsylvania] grinning groaning moaning meaning cleaning [Evaluating] meaning meaning cleaning cleaning preening screening preening screening preening screening screening preening prancing dancing dicing [Saying no] ricing spicing enticing icing aching baking balking caulking [Thinking one should change one's mind, thinking one should be capable of changing one's mind] biking hiking Swiss on rye hope pope lope dope grope gripe pipe pip pop [Still saying no] pap pep pup pep pap [No] pop pip pip pip [Not at all, inconceivable, beyond the pale] pop pog log pop log leg log pog peg pug pun sun done. "Pun sun done," the man said. "Pog peg pug pun." The man said. The man leaped. [No, we cannot make ourselves comfortable in our seats. No, it cannot be done.] The man raised his head. The man looked up into the sun.

MR. RODRIGUEZ IS

very rich, very rich is Mr. Rodriguez, but charities have found him to be benevolent. So it is. An old man. You. Mr. Rodriguez is very rich, but charities have found him. So it is. The gray stones. Mr. Rodriguez has been found, and he is very rich. So it is. So it is. Mr. Rodriguez has found charities. Mr. Rodriguez had been found but he was very benevolent and he had been rich but he was rich and he was found but he had been benevolent and rich but he had been found and rich and he had been. The ambulance and its crew. Mr. Rodriguez said, "Call me Señor." They called him Señor. They sent him letters. They sent him faxes. So it is. Tablets. They went to him by helicopter. He received them. They pleaded with him. He served them piña coladas and avocado. They entreated him. He served them platters of roasted jalapeños. They petitioned him. They used lawyers. They flew him around on Learjets. He ordered that they be served huevos rancheros, authentic style. They took him to rodeos and rock concerts. They said, "O Señor!" He drank margaritas. He drank tequila Sauza.

He drank Mezcal. They tried through secretaries. They tried through agents. He rode in limousines. They offered contracts. He sat for make-up. They called him "Señor." They called him, "El Grande." He learned his lines. They sent him contracts and scripts. He wore sunglasses. They lit him. They used diffusing screens so he would not be lit harshly. They had harsh thoughts but they used diffusing screens. So it is. They pulled the measuring tape up to his eyes. He rehearsed with them. They brought him Godiva chocolates. They sent publicity girls. He said, "Call me Señor." They blocked his moves. He made entrances. The cameraman said, "Oh! Oh, shit! Oh! Oh, hmm. Oh." Secretaries brought him Perrier. They served up croissants. They served up Brie. They served up melon and prosciutto. They served up seviche. They served up crabs. They served up gumbo. They served up tickets to major league baseball. He said, "Call me Señor." They begged him to do interviews. He rode into the sunset.

SCHMALLING WAS USHERED

through double doors into a bleak tunnel. There
was a magnificent view of the sunset. He whispered, "I haven't read any Joyce. At my age." There
was a magnificent view of the sunset. He swallowed the milky drink which Norma had concocted. The Four Horsemen of the Apocalypse are
Conquest, Slaughter, Famine, and Death. They
spent the day in their anemone garden, Schmalling
and she. There was a magnificent view of the sunset. He has traveled in the back of a limousine
since he was a child. A great river had once flowed
through the arroyo. I am one who does not sweat.
Drifters roamed among wrecked bicycles. You
can't truly enjoy a sport unless you know the basic
rules. Schmalling wanted to grow up to be a King,
or at least a Company President. Characteristics
of sharks: tiny brains, several sets of needle-sharp
teeth, not at all dangerous to _____.
Schmalling was ushered through double doors
into another, bleaker tunnel. There was a magnificent view of sunset. "Sharks: Not at All Dangerous
To _____." He said, "Call me Señor. Por

favor. Call me Señor." The exit was badly marked but they got off and rode all the way to Fairfax. Seven black crows. You can't really enjoy a sport unless you know the rules.

"AND TWO MORE,"

she said. She may well have had no teeth she had
so many teeth. But then I'm not sure about that. A
light was lit. The muscles of my palm. "You'll advise," she said, "You're wise, you'll advise, I'll com-
promise, it'll be a surprise. Call me Señorita." The
gray stones. The gray stones with gulls. I said to her,
"All out of sugar, Señorita! No baking possible."
We went for a sail. The dog sat up. On Saturday
night, as on all Saturday nights, Schmalling was
agonized. Schmalling was agonized, so he thought
the computer dating service would be wonderful.
He thought the computer dating service would be
wonderful, except that in fact he fell overboard.
He could not swim. We fished him out, Norma
and I, sobbing. We fished him sobbing. We, sobbing, fished him. Norma was wearing silk. Norma,
sobbing, wore silk, sobbing silk, her sobbing was
silken. I loved her in silk. I loved her in silk more
than anything, I loved her in silk. We fished him
out of that gelid black vacuity. O, God, crocodiles!
She was gorgeous in silk, she was something in silk.
The gray stones. She was brushing her hair. She

concocted something wonderful with cognac. I decided, looking at her, that at forty women become surrealistic. The gulls. She said, "I would give anything for goat's milk." My palm. The horse show was coming up Monday. Schmalling was whining uncontrollably on the pier. Schmalling had always told us he dreamt as a child he would grow up to become a King or at least a Company President but then the night before his high school graduation somebody came up and whispered that you can't really enjoy the game unless you know the rules. A blue balloon went up.

SCHMALLING CUT HIS FINGERNAILS

with clips like the ones Norma used, and it is even true that perhaps they were Norma's, and he bought six cauliflowers for a casserole remembering suddenly that his brother had to pay an adult fare since was twelve. Parking an impossibility, we ran. We lost ourselves in a labyrinth of lilacs. You can't always get what you want. I don't sweat. I, he, I, he. Schmalling cleaned himself with soap and sugar, a good method. Schmalling remembered that his brother, who had to pay an adult fare (since he was twelve), had painted three pictures: of a fire hydrant; of a split pomegranate; of a brown pot of tea. "Would you believe that I have not read?" Now I will tell you: the canyon was great, the arroyo was tiny. Beside the castle the sea was gray and there ran a hare. Beside the castle, the sea was all gray. Not a large hare, maybe not a hare, maybe something made of sand. Sand that moved. Beside, the castle was as gray as the sea. A light burned. The snow fell. The grimy gulls flew in and rested, and sat long, and lifted themselves from the gray stones to return again to the gray cloud that sat upon the gray sea.

Carceri d'Invenzione (Imaginary Prisons)

{1}

As the sun rose I was already seated beneath the great jacaranda in the climbing gardens of Abu Fellajin. A nondescript old crank wrapped in green rags shuffled my way, putting dead leaves into a canvas bag and chewing a walnut. "This way," muttered he, "sit yourself over here on this rock, and you will have a better view of what everyone in the world comes here to see, the glorious waterfall of Sapu Saddar, that will, if you dip into its pool, make you young again," and with a surprising strength, and perhaps something of a leer, he helped me to my feet and led the way to a broad cool stone that was made pink by the shimmer of sunrise. He knew his business, he'd spent his life driving some sort of tour bus. The rock overlooked an astonishing precipice, and the water that fell there was purple as it tumbled into the shadows of the giant ferns and scattered yellow hibiscus. "Sapu Saddar," the poet wrote, "Resting place of all who struggle,/ Her beauty as a tiger's waits in darkness."[1] The old

---

1 Te'va Rabindant Bugayam, episode XXXIV in *The Queenly Visions*, trans. William Arne and Patricia Longfellow Lear, London: Routledge and Kegan Paul, 1896.

man spoke again, now spitting a little. "There are many great marvels I could show you here. Nothing is unknown to me." There was an expression of cold sadness on his face but his gray watery eyes were painfully optimistic. Along a narrow pathway that climbed up past thick stands of rubber trees and twining creepers studded with liana he continued to shuffle forward. The air was hot and moist, opalescent. "All around us, poisonous lizards," he murmured—or was it, "All of us are poisonous lizards"?, my trouble with that language had always been with the referential use of the verb "to be"— and then, as though in an afterthought, but with a distracted and softened voice, he said something roughly like "So far withheld it is expressed, so interior it is everywhere, so silent it is deafening, so empty it is full." So empty it is full. So empty it is full. I adjusted my recorder, wondering if all this was getting onto the tape, or if not, how I would ever discern what this mysterious garble might have meant. Now, suddenly, there was a cave, its entrance mossy and very low, so that I had to fall to my hands and knees to contemplate it, and frankly it was terrifying, frankly terrifying. "So empty it is full," he said. "Yes, yes. Inside is the treasure. Inside, inside." It was hard to believe the secret cave could have been so close by. I looked up at him, at his flushed cheeks—too flushed. "Who are you?" He smiled without beneficence through lozenge lips. "I am the gardener. Here—my garden." I lowered myself almost to the ground, made way tentatively into the opening, that was barely large enough for one of the larger breed of dogs. "Yes," said he, "Inside. Inside." I felt myself losing form in the humid darkness, where I could see nothing. The recorder scraped on the ground. I thought I heard him say to me, "Have you not murdered? Is not this true?" but it might have been, "Have you the earth?" and I asked him to repeat himself, the damned language, but when I looked back, past my darkened shoulder, toward the gray-purple drop of daylight, the old man was gone. There was a smell of lichee or chrysanthemums, of fish, of dung, of berries, of cherimoya. Now I was completely inside. The place closed warmly around me like a cell. My hands hit a wet patch of ground covered with soft moss and I thought, what if there are snakes?, and then it all happened quite suddenly, as in the lighting of a match: a harsh voice whispered, "Damya," then something came over my head and everything was cramped darkness. I dreamed only that sharp arrows of color streaked across a jet-black sky, leav-

ing trails that vanished. Trails going nowhere. . . .
When I woke I was tied to a bed. Behind me were
gauze curtains, and the wind rushed onto my face
from a ceiling fan on a white ceiling. This was a ve-
randa of some kind. There was a putrid aroma, and
as I tried to move my eyes around—for my head
was tightly bound—I had the shameful sensation
that they had stripped me and washed me with
some sort of foul soap. A man in a blue uniform
approached and looked down into my face, lifting
a riding crop in front of my eyes. No native, this.
Perhaps from the North, Scandinavia, Leningrad.
He used the crop to tap my belly, and then lower, and still lower, as he asked, "Did you kill him,
then, the old man? Come, you can tell me. Did you
use a knife on him? There is no point in silence, we
will find out everything. Why don't you admit it
and save everybody a lot of bother. We have ways
of learning. We are very proficient." Two others
quickly pulled my knees apart and a pain shot up
my spine and there was darkness again.

•

To tell the truth, I cannot to this day recollect having killed—or even having known—anyone. A

clean wipe. They must have taken me in the middle of the night. I recollect no travel—through cities, through valleys. There is a flash of a road with shuddering poplar trees in headlights but that is all. I woke up here, far from home, and they tell me that I have been sentenced. There is a blue card nailed to the wall outside my cell, and on it in black ink is written, "Dephos carperon, tagmā filior nubet." These words mean nothing to me. They are also printed on the door to the cell block and outside in the exercise yard on a great red sign on the wall. When I ask what they mean, people ignore me. I notice that on work details it is not so much that I am guarded as that my person is watched, as though I supply by my appearance the wants of a great curiosity. I am judged, at any rate—it is easy enough to tell this by their eyes and the way, once they have seen me, they turn to whisper to one another. There are days when they line up in their brick-colored robes, on smelly tiers, cut by immense shadows, and comment upon me. At least once every day I am stripped bare and pointed at by these men who must constitute a race with small organs, for I am called "Water Melon," which of course may mean something different to them than it does to me, but they do laugh at me and hold their hands out to exemplify my enormity. I see them wagering. There is nothing I can do to escape their comments, their prying eyes, my feet being lashed to the paving on which I am forced to stand. There is nothing about me, my looks, my demeanor, even the way I breathe, that they do not reproach. Apparently the decision is yet to be made as to whether or not they will put me to death. Some real chance of that. A wealthy patron who has paid a small fortune for the privilege of being admitted to my cell has me stripped by two rough guards and proceeds to tickle my testicles with a small baton, then sits grumpily in the corner with a bowl of fat red noodles and something vaguely resembling chopsticks except corkscrew shaped. One of the possibilities is that I will live out my life here, under their gaze. We are on some sort of peninsula, I believe; some sort of promontory; and there are hideous storms. The dogs are squeamish about the thunder, and they quake and mewl like children. The dogs have been turned over to my care, and in fact I am called, generally, "Dogman" and sometimes even "Dog."

•

As they have been watching me I have been watching them and have discovered that they do not watch one another at all. In fact to one another they are undetectable, even as though invisible. When they talk, they look not past but directly through the body of the interlocutor, as though each is made of a kind of thickened smoke and in their conversations they might be speaking to the dead. They seem to refract through one another, and it must be admitted that their ideas are substantial, like clay or some other malleable substance, so that light, having to bend around their ideas, gives them solidity and shape, tiny sculptures, which last only a while before melting away. Their persons are insubstantial. I, however, appear to be the single one to have substance here. And having substance, I am the single one to be identified. For each other they do not have names. There is no aspect of myself which does not typify for them; and no utterance I can make which is not characteristic, they seem to think, of a peculiar being dressed as I am dressed, posed in my posture, positioned here, exactly as I am, upon these stones. These stones look as though they could be from Bardiglio but I have no idea where we are, and perhaps Bardiglio is half the world away. Once when I was a child I was led into a temple there and. . . . Well, a little later on we spent our time walking around the columns, sitting upon the plinths, reading from Maucus Didius Liminus and Proceptor Regalii, the sort of moldering old stuff one could dig up there. Here there is no library, but those old days are gone and I must be content with architectures and plants instead of books. Now, they huddle and confabulate about me. No one reaches out to touch me—I cannot see them but I would feel it—or gives me to think they wonder how I am today. There is no, "How are you? Are you feeling better?" But in truth, and according to a strange recipe the origin of which defeats my imagination, all is pain and all is also pleasure. I have lost track of time and have no idea whether my condition is improving or degrading. For me there being no today or yesterday I sometimes have the sensation that time is stopped. With the sound of what might be a violin or a shrill woodwind a tiny bright green snake creeps round a vine whilst the water pours like tourmalines over my hands from a source high in the mountain. The storms come irregularly but with what seems great frequency and there is an awful aura that anticipates them, the sky sickening green, the air stony and close. The dogs are incapacitated with grief. I know that I myself should be incapacitated and yet this knowledge, this tiny shred of connection to a world of my knowing, keeps me at a safe remove, gives me, perhaps, not exactly hope but reason to recollect such a thing as hope here in this brazen, this awkward and beautiful but unknowable world. Or to recollect the world outside that must have existed, after all, that platform from which I have been taken away, because surely here there is no hope. In a bowl that has been quite beautifully carved out of a rock I am brought a warm pabulum, it is grainy and tastes vaguely of papaya and corn. I should after several days find it tedious and unappetizing but queerly I do not. A woman passes in the mornings in a gray tunic. She is called Calandrea and something about the way she walks reminds me of you, whom I remember as I etch these words on the tablet they have given me (because of my demands, so repetitive and so obnoxious). My fingers begin to swell from the pain. Everything I say, and think to say here I address to you, doubting that you will ever see this. I know that doubt is born of hope and that if I had no hope there would be a blessed absence of doubt, but this does not change the fact that doubt is master of my thought and I have no reason to think this tablet will survive my presence in this cell (this cell which is five feet long and four feet wide and about seven or eight feet high, with a very tiny, basically useless window). I remember you in the morning when I see the woman called Calandrea and the pain of remembering you is so unbearable I pray that if she does not simply disappear she will do me the honor of slitting my throat, but she simply disappears.

•

I have been moved to a wooden chamber, with a bench. It is rather comely. There is of course no need for the place to be locked—it sits on a flat plain atop a high cliff; there is no imaginable escape—and so they do not trouble to lock it, nor is there need, now that I have been transferred to another group, or tribe, or gang, for my new keepers to abuse me in any way. So they are polite and even a little sweet. They can easily be certain I have no idea where I am. I remember distinctly a day—but I cannot say when this was: before a large bluish rock was deposited outside the narrow doorway I must pass through in order to get in here—when I

was on a playing field. I think it may have been in
the other place. Someone threw a ball high in the
air. The sky was the color of the ocean on a map in a
schoolroom, one of those old maps in one of those
old schoolrooms made all of varnished oak, a map,
or so it always seemed, painted by hand. I was running backward, squinting into the sun. That is all I
remember. I awoke here. I must have hit something
and fallen unconscious, or perhaps something else
happened altogether, because it was as though
suddenly I could not breathe and a dark curtain
descended, and when I could see again I was looking at this little piazza with that orange table. Two
men were playing draughts, the sky was avocado
green—they are not there now and the sky is dark-
er. I remember a vehicle speeding past, some kind
of chariot pulled by mules in ornate harnesses, I
think. I have no idea how old I am, only that I was
around thirty-two when I was in that other world
(because I remember, yet vaguely, celebrating my
thirty-second birthday and receiving a dart board
and a peanut pie), and they have given me no mirror, I am not even certain they have such a thing. I
certainly do not discern anything resembling a mirror in any dwelling in this place—I am allowed to
pass freely around—though I do remember, with

a fondness I cannot explain, that object we called a mirror. There being no pools, no slick surfaces, I cannot see what I look like, but the idea of seeing what I look like obsesses me even though the people in this place do not seem troubled by a similar idea. Nor do they stare at me all the time, as the other ones did, nor do they lack skin. The color of that is very hard to state. One sees patches of deep red, and then patches of flaming bright yellow-orange, and then, if the light is right, spots of a kind of peacock green. They look into one another's faces vacantly, not really in order to see anything but just in order to signal the direction of their regard. One imagines they find it impossible to conceive that you can be seen. They have the aggressive, tickling stance of those who touch the world without ever being touched. At any rate, I cannot see whether I have grown older by a great deal or only months; and in truth, I cannot recall what I looked like even at the other place, on the day I ran backward to catch that horrifying and beautiful thing, that lure, falling out of the sky. They have provided me with a little purple fish in a dark bowl that seems to have been carved out of some mammoth root, and this being swims around and around seeking what is just ahead of him. Sometimes he hovers and seems to think about his watery world, but I suspect he is not thinking, only waiting, and as I try to imagine myself being like him he taunts me by flying away from my gaze into an abrupt little shadow that is impossibly far from my hand.

•

The men have come in tens and twenties down the great stone steps at twilight, clutching walking sticks and cloaked in thick robes. I am informed that I have been found guilty, and that there was no question in the tribunal about my guilt. Having said all this, they depart. It is true that I do not know of what crime I have been found guilty, or even what constitutes a crime in this place. I scanned their faces to see if they held a hint of my future, but no man regarded me as anything but the person he was talking to. My pulse sped up and I began to panic, but I forced myself to regulate my breathing, I thought of the taxonomical names of the lower vertebrates, Elasobranchii nocturnalis, Siphonops paulensis minor and Siphonops paulensis major, Fetureansis temporalus, and also birds, Poicephalus giulelmi, Gouldian finches, the class of ravens, the fan-tail, the Australian, the pseudobranchial, and the many variants of the date palm, the "Monastery date," the Omani, the luscious Khadrawi, then numbers of our arcane mathematics, finally words lifted bodily from their beds in the dead of night, kelp, the eye of the ostrich, roasted pistachio, girder, flank. In the market I was able to procure more food for my fish by paying for it with my blood. A nurse took my blood into a phial, in a small rude laboratory. I found her quite mechanical, and searched in vain for an expression of concern as she let my blood flow into her container (which was dirty, but the tube she had stuck into me was clean, or so I think), but as far as she was concerned I was only the source of a material good and she had no reason for being anything but efficient. The blood also allowed me to buy vegetables—some oblong gray objects roughly like potatoes—and I was given combustible materials from which to make a tiny fire to roast them. They cooked slowly, but they were very good indeed, with a tangy flavor and a soft meat inside. I am very weary and also, it seems, by comparison with the prisoners around me, wealthy.

•

The woman they call Calandrea has been identified to me as the Chief Presiding Magistrate and she has presented herself to question me. No etiquettes or formalities. She used a tiny keyboard device designed ideally for her four-fingered hands, and I had to note her glistening flying fingers. Great tranquility about her eyes, broad cheeks, a serene arrogance one could only admire. I could vaguely imagine sculptors going mad to see her. What, she wanted to know, could I tell of the place in which I had been born, my youth, my work, my loves, my library? What could I tell of my race, my passion, my intentions, my predilections, my geographical experience, my friendships? Of all these I retain no memories at all, I merely sense diffuse colors, and so I apologized and asked her, "Have you done something to my mind?" but she regarded this question as discernably strange, and made a pouting moue which was more than beautiful upon her lovely face, and she ruffled her fine gray gown. What, then, could I tell her about my business associations, my contracts, my strategic plans, my filing system? "Think of your body," she said. "Think of parts of your body. Do you have memories attached to your body parts? Your arms? Your hands? Your eyes?" For these last words she halted and struggled, because they do not have what we would call arms or hands or eyes. It is as though her lips were carved of pearwood and her nostrils fashioned by Michelangelo, I remember thinking, quite briefly, but the joke was that I could think of pearwood and of Michelangelo but didn't know what or who they were. It was only as though a word or phrase had been dictated to me, and I could rehearse it: "It is as though her lips were carved of pearwood and her nostrils fashioned by Michelangelo." She tapped me on the shoulder several times, rhythmically, but as to whether that was a sign or signal, I couldn't say. "Martvat" was another utterance she made, many times, and it, too, was a mystery.

•

They have decided to move me yet again. I hope and trust I have not been a burden, for these folk have been inordinately civil to me, even, one might say, friendly. I am told I will be drugged and will remember nothing of the voyage. I am led past a cell where the Chief Presiding Magistrate is working on someone else, "Think of parts of your body. Do you have memories attached to your body parts? Your arms? Your hands? Your eyes?" There is a van and in it a white stretcher and then an injection.

{2}

I am now in a place bounded by vast fields and massive plinths. The sweet beery smell of new-mown barley is in the air. The people here are scarcely larger than I am, and yet the plinths are monumental, great slabs of granite or some other very even and smooth stone laid into henges, and I cannot imagine how without technology—because of technologies there are no traces here, beyond what the medical practitioners use—they can have managed to effect such a world. People walk hither and yon with tablets of a substance like stone, yet not stone, beneath their arms and a certain radiance surrounding their heads. I was not allowed to bring the fish but they have given me another in a new bowl, a green slender fish. The people reside in low wattle-and-daub structures with thatched roofing and yesterday I heard two of them talking about the expense of the insurance on structures like these: you have to take out a full second policy on the roof itself. It seems they spend almost a third of their income on insurance. Outside the village—I would call it that, yet it has no central area, no fountain, no place of worship—is a large smokehouse and they smoke meats brought in from the forest. They smoke hill venison—that is their name for it, I have never seen the animal itself—and hedge grouse and a wild boar similar to ours but with much smaller tusks, partridges which scramble among the hedgerows bordering the forests, field snipe, woodcock, black-tailed rabbit. I believe that in coming here I have been moved further inland, because I cannot smell the lilt of sea salt in the air and the few birds I see are like mountain birds—condors, hawks, peregrines of sorts. I am regarded almost as a sacred object by these people. They do not touch me, and if by accident one of them brushes against me he backs away in fear, bowing low and muttering something incomprehensible. I spend my days doing absolutely nothing but walking through the village and sitting on stones, very smooth pinkish stones, and the local people assemble to gawk at me. Sometimes one will try to reach out with a twig to graze my limbs. The others slave away at chiseling rock, making large wattle-and-daub panels from reeds they dry and bird droppings they mix with rainwater, or birding, hunting, cooking, building shelters. There are some children, not very many, and they race after one another among the trees and then sit for long hours in groups of two or three tying up one another's hair in fancy patterns and smearing colored unguents on their friends' faces. I have not at any point here been treated as though I ought to be working and, indeed, they seem not to notice at all as I stand aside to watch them in their labors. In this habitation I have seen fewer than a dozen children. And it is strangely silent, beyond the bird calls. They make a hissing occasionally but nothing one would call language.

•

A young man and woman walked off together beyond the plinths yesterday, and I followed them, looking often behind me to see if anyone was following me. They went off toward the ebony forest, down a little inclination, behind a great green rock, and tucked themselves among some high ferns—giant ferns towering over our heads. Into the woods they continued to march on what had once, ages ago, been a pathway but was now almost completely grown over with thick roots and entangled vines dropped from some high branches. They stepped carefully, over decaying logs and across tiny rivulets with me following, and they muttered vowel sounds that I could not make out, difficult to render here but something like "ghwohhhhh" and "ahhahhhaiii." No one, least of all I myself, would have surmised what my purpose could be in following them, save to discover an answer to a question I could not declare myself to know. I realized it was probable they would make love and that I urgently wanted to see this, but I cannot imagine what my purpose could have been in this desire as normally in my life, as you will know better than anyone, I am a shy and very modest man. Surely not to see *them* as persons, possibly to see them as types—so it seems to me now. But the truth is that as I experienced this desire, at that very moment, I could not explain it to myself or to anyone. I knew that they would engage in a violent production, silent or not so silent, and that they would return without the device of strategy or yearning and I return having seen the act but being able to make nothing of it, for in the end it is an act that has no meaning outside of itself. The vision of the complicated twisting, extending, and contracting I admit I expected, because like everyone I have ever known I have a terribly limited imagination. They arrived at a dark part of the woods and dropped their voices. The sound of something rushed up suddenly and they disappeared between two mossy boulders, and I behind a third. I waited a little and, catching sound of their receding steps on the leaves of the forest floor, went after them again. There was a waterfall and a lagoon, under a parting of the trees. Marvelous. Some guava trees on the far side, heavy with yellowing fruit, the lagoon itself jade green and untroubled but for the intrusion of the waterfall. The sunlight shone full down on the water. Quickly they undressed and plunged into the waters, screaming with delight. The male came up to the female and threw his arms around her playfully. She made as though to fight him off, giggling, and swam behind the tumbling water where I could vaguely make out some flat stones. He came onto the bordering beside the fall rocks and made his way carefully around it to meet her. I did not know where to go to see them better, because now the water crashing into the pool was all I could see with clarity, and a myriad yellow flies hovering in a kind of mist over the green pool. But now they were re-emerging from the waterfall and gliding together into the pool, stroking to the center where the light was brightest. I wondered if they would attempt a coupling in the water, or whether they would come onto land, or if—and the possibility of this hurt me, it seems so odd to confess although it was so automatic at the time—in some spontaneous flickering of great power they could have finished already, out of my sight. They laughed, she throwing her head back and he catching at the center of her back with his hand. They were edging toward me, I took it because the footing under them was slippery. I was low to the ground behind some thick ferns grown up into a wall, and where flat rocks bordered the water. They were on the rocks now, immediately in front of me, the bodies glistening in perfection. Suddenly the man stood up, his mouth agape, his black eyes peering at the trees behind me and his swollen member purple and ready. I could hear him catch his breath, they were so near. I heard rustling, but too late. Arms seized me from behind, tightened upon me like straps in a machine, and voices were hissing, and the man laughed in delight and the woman laughed with him as the soldiers lashed my wrists and took me back to the village, hissing all the way. I was locked into a sort of wagon and driven away that same night, over rough roads, and it was cold and the stars were legion up above. I heard those two young laughs trailing after me for hours, imagined she would expand and he link into her with images of my fear-stricken face goading their thoughts. The man who drove the wagon was of a different species, brown-eyed and squat as I could see through a tiny barred window, and when, once, he turned to me and offered hot broth he said, "Nobilu." His voice made me afraid, although it is a fact that until this moment I had not at any point experienced fear in the place from which he was extracting me. I worried about where we might be headed, realized with a mixture of black fear and blinding doubt the simultaneous weight and weightlessness of the fact that I could not foresee a destination. Before this, if the future had never seemed palpable it had also not seemed foreboding, but that this man had a solicitous tone when he spoke to me chilled me to the depths. "Will they put me to death?" I heard myself say, not that I thought he would comprehend, and indeed, these were just so many sounds chained within a voice I had forgotten how to recognize so much time had passed without me speaking. Why, if men and women coupled, were there no children in that place?, I wanted to ask him somehow, as well, but kept silent. And who were these people? But the wagon had stopped moving and the driver, leaning over me, seemed to dissipate in a fog. I caught my breath. The bundles of hay that were in the wagon, that had left strands entangled in my hair, disappeared before my eyes and I was standing on a platform in a great obsidian palace under moonlight. I could hear and only dimly see a river, and the High Priestess was swimming in the darkness with her handmaidens blowing flutes, and I looked down and saw that my feet had been laced into military sandals and that embossed golden plates were on my thighs and chest. On a table were platters with honey cakes and great amethyst goblets of ale. I thought I heard celli and tambourines. A dog barked far in the distance. In a courtyard were a thousand soldiers, raucously shouting and throwing spears at targets made of hacked up roast boars and drinking from silver pitchers and bearing massive clusters of grapes on rods slung between their shoulders. The High Priestess was borne into the temple on an alabaster throne, and she said to me, "Prepare thyself."

•

This figurine was dark, or else they had smeared her all over with something that would make her skin shimmer like the scales of a snake, and she was very tall, and on her lips they had painted a shining and dark purple coating, almost black, like the plumes of certain exotic birds, and this color was also on her nails, which she kept moving in front of my face as her eyes, black, regarded me without a blink, so that I myself trembled. She blew some flavored smoke into my face, but now I have awakened in a garden, where youths promenade naked and I am unable to move, lashed to a tree with thousands of filaments as delicate as corn silk, a true Gulliver. But as I look with more concentration—as straining my eyes is practically the only action available to me—I can see that in fact I am not lashed at all, I have somehow become part of the tree. The young people seem utterly unconscious of their nakedness, but as I look more closely I see that they are not humans but fawns. The flowers are growing around them even as they breathe. A light rain is falling. There is a sound of delicious moaning in the air, a trumpet sound. I am falling. I am falling into a pit and the air is warming.

•

Men are distributed around me in a circular chamber, seated on stools, writing in great ledgers with quills. There must be two hundred of them. Boys in tailcoats are racing from desk to desk carrying what looks like money from one man to another. The amounts changing hands here must be in the tens of millions. One of the boys—a young male fawn—stops near me to chat with his friend, a redhead. "How much?" says this first, and the redhead responds, fast as a button, "Two hundred and eighty." "Million!" says the first, his eyes bulging. The second raises his eyebrows: "No no! More!" You can hear the quills scratching all the way up to the ceiling, like eagles in cliff caves; there is a round skylight of many-colored glass. The boys—the young male fawns—are out of breath. I am suddenly become one of the men with quills, seated on my habitual stool, but I cannot remember what I am supposed to be calculating here, or how I became what I am, and I look up at the many-colored glass and the colored light trickling down through it in stately bars, and the boy fawn who is waiting for me seems bored, but I have no idea how much to offer him and he says, "At least half a million," so I look around but there is nothing. "I'll take blood," he says, and offers one of those little phials and some (clean) equipment. He seems very interested in my hand as he draws blood from my forearm, the knuckles, the mound of flesh at the base of the thumb. Behind my desk there is a little door and he leads the way through it, saying hoarsely, "Follow." We go into a small room furnished with a divan and a chandelier. "Sign," he says, offering a receipt printed on orange paper, and I sign it in what is distinctively tangerine orange ink, there is an ink-well, but as I write I cannot see any ink forming my name. He is looking around, perhaps furtively. I am suddenly reading his mind. He wants more money than I can possibly make for him with my blood, what I have done is to rouse his hunger. He steps back and looks at me, his pink tongue showing. He opens my mouth and looks at my teeth and I can smell his licorice breath. "We had better have you come out and sign the rest," says he, and he leads the way back out into the transaction chamber where there is a huge dossier on my desk with each document neatly marked off with little colored flags at each place where I must sign. He slowly rubs my shoulders while I sign, but he is not attempting to produce pleasure, he is attempting to induce a rhythm to increase the efficacy of my signing, and I am conscious of the pricking pain in my right arm where he took the blood. The documents seem countless and I am signing dizzily, the ending of my name laced to the beginning of my name flowing to the end of my name becoming the beginning of my name, all invisible. I begin to lose sense of my name, there are so many pieces of paper. My name is soon only a chain of swirls made with a quill. "Keep signing," says my fawn clerk, hastily rubbing my shoulders. Then he rushes off and gives the pile of signed documents to another clerk, who rushes off. My desk is bare. Now my clerk is back and this time he is staring into my face and laughing at me mirthfully, throwing back his head. "Filling and then filling or filling and also filling and also filling and usually filling or filling," I hear someone say, and I am sitting on a long polished wooden bench with all the clerks. The Chief Recorder is wheeling a trolley collecting documents and ringing a bell. Tomorrow, it seems, they are going to marry me. That must be what the fawn was laughing about. They have signed the necessary affidavits and it is sufficient that the affidavits contain the fawn signatures even without my own, because the affidavits in question are not the forms I signed, and indeed I now forget the signed forms as I am obliged to concentrate on reading the affidavits for errors of spelling or punctuation (of which I find not a one).

I am to be disrobed ceremonially by fawn boys and washed by these clerks in fragrant showers and dressed in chaplets of purple and a gilded wreath will be fixed onto my head by a device like a screwdriver or an awl that is mounted in an armature in a shimmering green high coil, and I am told the experience will be strangely pleasurable. They will take me to a stage and there will be a huge audience. I will have to memorize a series of stanzas and then I will be carried away with my betrothed—I cannot imagine her, they keep all hints away from my ears and make no suggestions to me—I will be carried away to a boat beneath a canopy on the river and rowed among preening blue river birds while fires are lit and there is a sweet cantorial and platters of steamed urchins are passed with mangoes and slivered marsh pineapples and boiled quail eggs. They are coming with the equipment now because they want more blood. The nuptial barge will bear us to an island and from the island it is rumored we will be taken off by aircraft, but the question of governments has come up and it now seems much more likely there will be no aircraft and no island but a direct passage across to the mainland.

•

They have sent a shabby looking man to take my blood this afternoon, a second-level clerk by the look of him. He seems to have been drugged he moves so lethargically but the shirts he has brought me in exchange for the blood seem well made and of decent cloth and he is friendly enough, though once he gets going a little too talkative. I do not loathe people, far from it, but I have a severe acoustic trouble—it has been with me as long as I remember: I cannot bear to listen to what is not euphonious. This, coupled with my long history of studying Latin manuscripts, has forced me into a position of retreating from language that tortures by the excruciating indirectness of its incomplexity, its inaccuracy, its asymmetry, or its failure in prolonged spiels to find the exquisiteness of depth. This man quotes game scores. He utters opinions about politicians—a gender about which there seems to me no point in holding opinions because everyone has an opinion and all the opinions are basically the same opinion. From this man, who becomes more acutely informative as the minutes pass, I learn that in fact I have not been married. The illusion of matrimony is only one of the many illusions cultivated and fostered in this place, and is indeed their principal illusion, because by means of it the hapless prisoner, convinced of the reality of a mutuality of affection and concern, is sealed off from awareness of his isolation. In this way he is preserved, like a peach in brandied honey, and his visit attenuated without stress. I tried to understand this strange idea, because it did not seem to me either obvious or natural that the wardens would wish to keep prisoners for as long as possible, given that upkeep represented a huge cost. Perhaps, I suggested, keeping prisoners optimistic increased the chances that they would feel encouraged to part with vital information. But no, the wardens were not in the slightest interested in gaining information from their prisoners. "First," said my bleeder, "we could never be certain of the quality of the information we were harvesting, given that you would not be yielding it voluntarily. We would have to be suspicious, and suspicion is itself a corruption of the quality of information. You know, that's what Wabble was always saying when he ran for Principalium last spring. I always liked Wabble, honest, forthright fellow. Good at the bat, too. But that aside, you aren't here to give us information and my colleagues and I aren't gleaners." I mar-

veled at this, and asked what, then, the prisoners
were supposed to give. "It's as Wabble always said
in those fabulous speeches. You are not here to
give. But that goes without saying. As I told you,
we are not gleaners." So they did have "gleaners,"
but he was not one of them. I began most seriously
to wonder about my condition, in a way I had not
wondered before: although this was not a man of
power, and although he was by no means the most
intellectual or precise of thinkers, nevertheless my
friend spoke with a certain offhanded rhythm of
authority; and moreover, what motive could he
possibly have had for lying to me when I was so ab-
jectly and thoroughly in his control? So, why was
I here if not to give? The question kept troubling
me. It became a kind of patterned toile, this question, covering all the surfaces of my consciousness.
But then I saw it, even as his lips moved to make
the answer. They had come to the end of their teth-
er, producing so smooth a world, and so luxurious
a life—as creatures of this sort might understand
luxury—that half the population was unnecessary
to the survival of the other half. They needed the
prisons to hold off an upset of the order, and to
provide work; nothing more. I was here in order
to be kept from claiming the piece of cake—really,

the bowl of liana pulp pudding—that somebody else wanted to eat. "I could do your injection now as well, if you'd like. Because, as Wabble always said, and it's such a pity he wasn't elected, because he would have been superb—'Everything always!'" The pudding had actually been baked, and took the rather strange form of a gaufrette that was fed to people like me by means of a neurostimulator—a complicated technique, to be sure—once every other day, on a timetable that had been worked out by a nutritionist secreted away somewhere. I had not been married in my other life, and now that they had abandoned the idea of marrying me here the decision had been taken to administer me soon with a drug that would lead me to conceive of myself as a married man, and in that state of consciousness, it was believed, I would be happy, indeed fulfilled. "Also," he offered, "we could do a seminal extraction for realism." Certainly, I was speechless. And then he assured me that regardless, there would be cushions and furniture, simulated voyages, lasting companionship—or at least the impression of all these. "You could set up a time-table for seminal extractions," he said a little eager-ly, "if you liked. Or—." But the "or" never came. Someone was playing a flute elegiacally. They were proficient at giving you to believe someone was interested in you. They needed to keep you alive as long as possible because it was far cheaper to maintain a prisoner than to capture a replacement for one who had died of loneliness. They could handle inoculating you against disease but not smoothly manage what you would do to yourself through neglect or imagination if you realized no one else was there. No, they could never account for, or design for, what we would do to ourselves through imagination. "We could have the extraction done by a young man, or a young woman, or both together," he said optimistically, perhaps overdoing it. "It intensifies the illusion, you know. The *blethoi* are all very experienced." So the fawns had a name. He went out and came back after a few moments with a goldfish in a bowl, this one pearl blue. At the bottom, under a pathetic wisp of some pinkish kelplike substance, were some flat stones, polished and gray. "I have one of these," he said, "just like this one. I find these stones very good for meditating, in case you like to meditate. You've given me plenty of blood, I'm quite happy. The fish is covered, and so is the bowl. And I probably owe you, to be honest, so tomorrow I'll bring a little book of pictures of people who were famous once."

{3}

I have not been able to write a word for six weeks.
They have transferred me to a station in the north,
and my pens and notebooks were confiscated and
only yesterday returned to me (with pages missing). It was in the middle of the night I was taken.
They came with weapons raised and said I should
hurry and dress, and there would be time to pack
one small bag; but the writing materials were to
be left behind. It was a kind of bus they brought
me on, quite frigid because the heating was out of
order, and the territory we had to move through
was a tundra with wide rocky plateaus, the road
scratched into a furrow of granite. The seats of the
bus were like blocks of ice, and outside there was
blue moonlight and frost, and ice upon the trees,
you could almost feel the heavy branches sagging
with it. I suddenly came down with a horrid attack of vertigo, the whole world seemed to twist
and sink away from me for hours on end, even if
I closed my eyes, and only if I twisted my head
down onto my left shoulder did the frightening
effects diminish. I had to sit like this almost the

whole length of the journey, and then for several days more once we arrived. It passed as suddenly as it had come, and there was a yellow aura which was warm and almost intoxicating. Here there are cabins made of a local wood like spruce that smells heavenly, and one can light a fire and make a good soup with tiny perfect potatoes and very rich, dark greens that grow in abundance. A violinist plays in the evenings, a man from Brazynn, so they say. I can write letters but I have no one to write to. I can read a frayed copy of Vityupovkal with which they have provided me, the pages all but coming away from the glue. It's a boring book but I amuse myself by imagining the sentences placed next to one another in a different order. I think sometimes it would be enchanting to cut them out with a razor blade and paste them into my writing book that way, but who might not come after me to this place wanting something to read and be cheated by my act of creativity? "Ah glorious spring, when we kill pike!" the book begins—that sort of thing, direct style, farmer's mentality—and there is a particular sentence, "The girls had nothing to do now but wait for them to return, because Tyus Mladyusot had commanded that the men had four excursions to make before they could settle into marriages," just that, and I was thinking it would be really nice to line it up against "Ah glorious spring, when we kill pike!" The inquisitorial sessions—the village manager has been trying to persuade me to call them "debates"—are the Fourth and the Seventh days at one (they use an eight-day calendar), and they go on for hours. I am strapped into a kind of divan. They perfume the air with something spicy and oceanic, and they ask a lot of questions about filing practices in the other place and who had authorization to see which memoranda—truly, the stuff I have forgotten in the best of faith. My cellmate—I have a cellmate!—is a Galifarzian named Tcherllinng and he is forever washing his hands and grinning and trying to make jokes that I frankly don't find funny. He gets letters from his son, and reads them over and over and then puts them under a pile of stones to flatten them and ties them together with an old shoelace. They took me in for a special "debate" last night after dinner. Some photographs of army people had arrived and been turned into slides and they flashed them on a screen and asked if I could identify anyone. I didn't recognize a single face. They had wrapped my wrists with rubber sleeves filled with water and connected to wires. "Nonsense," the chief medical technician chuckled as I denied face after face—he had quite a warm chuckle, quite friendly—"Nonsense, some of these people you have been quite intimate with. One of them is your cellmate." I looked again and yes, it was Tcherllinng, whom they had dressed up with a hat too big and floppy pants that turned him into a sad clown. I'm sorry, said I, but with the others I just don't remember. My mental faculties are weak. I find I cannot remember much. And this answer didn't seem to please anybody because they scribbled very quickly and grumbled to one another, and the doctor said again, this time scathingly, "Surely you recognize *this man*?" He backed up to a slide of a balding fellow about sixty, with cold blue eyes and a scar over the bridge of his nose. "*Surely you can put a name to him?*" I sat there with the pressure pumping my arms, stunned by helplessness and even a kind of lightheaded mirth. "Surely a name comes to mind, some kind of a name, when you see this *face*?" The more I stared at the cold eyes and the flat nose and the thick lips, the more I began to fear that I really did know him, and that he had had some terrifying relation to my past, and yet, swim through faces as I did, this one just did not attach itself to anything. I thought it would be very nice to be able to eat some chocolate, which they did not provide, which they had never provided, none of them in any of these places. And I wondered who that could be outside in the snow playing two chords over and over on a balalaika.

{4}

After the ceremony of the blindfolding and the injection I felt myself being lowered into a box lined
with thick smooth blankets and then picked up. I
must have blacked out then, because when I awoke
I was here. It must be a grand château, judging by
the character of the room in which I find myself.
The ceiling is extraordinarily high—perhaps eighteen feet or more. There is a baroque molding
that runs through the full oval of the ceiling and
drops down as well, to surround the Louis XIV
marble fireplace which is the color of yellow caviar. The walls are painted a very dark peach color,
the sunset blush on the peach, and the floor is par-
queted. One of the walls is covered top to bottom
with toile de Jouy in a watery blue print of camels.
The furniture is Louis XIV as well, and remark-
ably well preserved, upholstered some in the most
flamboyant citron and the rest in very dark, almost
black, forest green silk brocades. Every morning
at ten (a golden clock on the mantle, shaped like a
three-master at sea with cannons and rigging, too!)
they bring black coffee—the real thing!—in a little

Sèvres service with ground sugar in a special bowl made of malachite. I am allowed to walk out and down the corridor which is lined with gilt-framed portraits taller than I am, past doors painted moss green and fluted with gold, and each room I encounter is not an *endroit* but a memory. There is the room of the Luschtchantzky Park, where I was wheeled as an infant swarmed by the branches of winter trees at which I stared upwards, and the room of the concert hall of Pogrebinza, with the great black piano on the vast stage. Touftoy played that: Skriabin, Chopin, Bach. There is the library of Ilyutin, an ocean of red bindings metrically gilded and ascending on balconies up, up, up, up, up so far one loses sight. A colossal chandelier there, the size of a small carousel. One of the rooms has the quality of a university, one of a hospital, another is that of my friend Staskin-Voux who caught the fever in his twenty-second year and died very swiftly. It was a horror, because when I last saw him he was gray when the sun ducked behind a cloud and sallow when it came out and very gaunt and his eyes were pleading. I sat with him, I remember, and we read. And then he was white and I mopped his head, but it was too late. It was too late. Another room is a vegetable market in Marrakech, yes. The sound of tambourines. The rooms go on. There are people in the rooms, but some are dead and some are only figments, rather like characters in a book. They don't any of them recognize me. In some of the rooms are architectural configurations or décor that somehow seem very dear to me—a marbled staircase, a sconce in an olive green room, a rumpled bed, an upstairs window looking down onto a woodpile where a man is struggling with a saw day and night, a huge wood stove with a high smoke pipe going through the ceiling, black and comforting, where ice skates have been put to dry, a cellar room piled with boxes upon one of which sits an ancient typewriter whose keys are so heavy it hurts to press them. I find that each day, as I muster the energy and go out to walk the corridors, there have sprung still more corridors, and corridors opening from these corridors, and more rooms. This palace is enormous beyond enormity, but there are no windows looking out into the grounds. A staircase leads up to yet another corridor and up there are rooms with musical instruments in glass-fronted cabinets, and rooms with clothing piled on tables, and a room with chairs lined up all round in a great circle against the walls—these walls the depressing charcoal color of chickens' blood after slaughter—

and there are people seated in the chairs and no one is moving. There is a room in which boys and girls are tossing green and yellow beanbags up into the air, shouting words I cannot decipher, "Blafa! Ratho! Svart! Vlafat! Rathu!"

•

I realize that in all these places I have been to, island after island, when people speak in my hearing I do not understand them. No hope at all of understanding. I hear the words and repeat them rote, making tiny mouth sounds that resemble what one might hear from a calliope. Not a word, not a sentiment is clear, or ever was.

•

The Director-General called me in. "Our purpose," said he, lighting a cigar, and only after I had made myself sufficiently comfortable in a beautiful but frail wooden chair that had no curvatures, "is to render indistinguishable from each other the world you brought with you into this place and the world we have given you. Our purpose is to free you to mingle at leisure in the society you have left behind while still you remain here with us, in this very establishment. This," he continued, sniffling, "is a little like killing you for your own good. Yet it's also a new horizon we're opening to you. There is nowhere for you to go, because you must go everywhere. Our purpose is to increase the size of the château until it incorporates everything you need. We have finite but unbounded resources." That was a little speech I could not confess to understand completely. I had a flash of a room containing a field in which a horse was running. "Our purpose is to help you relive your history." The horse was straining, sweating, water was coming from its eyes. A photograph of Kazimiercz, or of Eddesley, they always looked so much alike, a tinted photograph, and he was reaching up and touching the brim of his fedora. "Our purpose is to bring to you your own past, as a kind of service. We wish you never to lack for your past, but also to depend upon us for having it. We will remodel the château extensively. We will take down walls and make the rooms much larger, and we will add wings." He gestured with his hand, his rather hairy hand, in the air, showing how he would make the rooms more expansive and add corridors filled with rooms that were more expansive still. He wore a white wig and silks (lavender silks). He looked rather like a dish of candies. On the eleventh floor—for they had added seven stories just since my arrival—there was a room in which my old friend Paulot lay upon his bed next to a small table with a reading light. "We will have to get going soon," Paulot said, and it was winter outside, and both his mother and his father had not yet come home from work. "It's getting late." He stood up and yawned and put his shoes on while I watched him with care, and said somewhat nervously, "You're coming, aren't you?" And he went out. I did not follow him, and I do not know where he is now. That was the last I saw of him. I lay for a while on the bed and looked at the book Paulot kept there, *The Lost Child*. It was well worn and I thought perhaps I'd read it, but when I opened to the first page suddenly the room was gone, and the château with it, as though in a breath, and I was on a street in London, Kingsway near enough to High Holborn in the mist that comes after a rain, and I was staring into the vitrine of a bookshop. There rested *The Lost Child* upon a little spotlit reading stand and behind me someone came up smartly tapping an umbrella on the pave and said, "Time."

•

I have been seeking a vale of peace and pleasure here in my cell. Long meanders through crevices in the dull enshadowed rocks have led to dried up rills, bald pockets of purple-black rock, but I have persevered within the carapace of my longing self, hunting in the nights, past the sentries, through all my numbered chambers. Through the chambers mapped on my numbered maps all hung in the file room from floating beams that can be pulled down or let up I have hunted, and have seen pleasures once tasted long ago now rendered as ciphers. I have hunted for pleasures and found indices of pleasure, yet always the azure-white sky floats outside my window. They will not release me into the courtyard where the sea air mixes with the southernwood and the daffodil. Far beyond the promontory, whales are blowing in the sound, yet I am caught up in the hunt within, hoping to snag the flying beast. I climb into my lighthouse. They tell me I have been here for so many years they have lost count. Every rising sun is a new medallion. Waves my punctuations.

•

In the library, they have three books, torn, none complete, and of one there are but three pages. I read them over and over, imagining to myself the pages before and the pages after. One book contains instructions on the mass production of suet cakes. One book contains the sentence, "I am a man without a country in a country without men." I sit for hours as the gulls bray and repeat this, "I am a man without a country in a country without men." A country in a country. Without a country in a country. I am a man. They come in the afternoon with a tray of woven grasses and distribute candied plums, which I adore beyond measure and which are glorious beyond description, red, glowing, sweet. In the third book there are aphorisms. "Sheep always follow a good shepherd." "The clock that does not strike still waits." "Knowledge is not knowing that one does not know." I repeat this last a hundred times, until it is a mantra. Two nurses bring me into a green room and strip off my outer robe and my inner robe. They have clipboards. One applies cold steel instruments to my chest and back and the other moves around me singing a little mantra of her own, "It's not an emotional problem but a brain disorder." Who is she speaking about? She leans over me, muttering, "Yes, yes, nothing, nothing." What, nothing? What, yes, yes? "What do *you* think?" says the first nurse, rather the more bovine of the two. The other, who far too much resembles a llama, responds, "Don't know, *you*?" It's not an emotional problem but a brain disorder. Knowledge is not knowing that one does not know. Sheep always follow a good shepherd. "We must make an arrangement," the first says, "Arrangement is all." *Le décor c'est tout.* The chilling lozenge of a stethoscope finds its way to my underarm. They place me in a device which anchors my head as lights are flashed in many colors in front of my eyes, blue, green, mauve, amber, blue, blue, green, mauve, mauve, amber, amber. I am to discern which lights are most prevalent, the green ones or the amber ones. I go into the woods and hunt for moss on the biggest stones, greenest moss, and driest, and try to sit comfortably for an hour to meditate and collect myself, knowledge is not knowing that one does not know, and the smell of rutting animals is around me and rotten leaves and pine needles, and it is a brain disorder not an emotional problem. I hear a voice telling me the pigs were here I am sure the pigs were here but the pigs have been castrated and when they are castrated the squeals are horrible. The two nurses have turned away to talk and seem unaware that I am here. They have made tea and are chatting amiably. I am shivering. One of them, the one who could be a wildebeest, turns and tells me they are not going to bring me clothing, but instead they are going to put me into a boat and take me out into the sound and where the whales are blowing throw me into the water once and for all. "Once," she says, "and for all." She watches me and makes a notation. I am warned that they will make two pie crusts, one for the top, one for the bottom. Oxidation is important. Sheep follow a good shepherd. The pinball machine was defective at the factory, beyond repair. The pinball machine had amber and green lights, and mauve, and pink. I am sure that the pigs were here. Asparagus have been harvested. It's not an emotional problem it's a brain disorder. Robed again and taken back to the library. Smell of asparagus cooking. Someone in a pink shirt is obsessively needling the pinball machine. They have put the asparagus into a sort of pie, one crust on top, one on the bottom. There is a little picture of an iceberg torn and crumpled in a corner of the floor. It's a brain disorder. I can hear Lieutenant General

Kidron playing Strauss upstairs on the old organ or
if not Strauss his imitator Wagenheim. It's not an
emotional problem. No one has found the solution
but I am told in a brief communiqué from Berlin
that varnish may be the key and there is great moment to the elaboration of a toccata. I'm quite certain it is all code, and I retreat to the security of the
thought that knowledge is not knowing that one
does not know, the clock that does not strike still
waits, but still I must search the control panel for
every possibility, convinced, utterly convinced that
if only I touch the correct buttons in the correct sequence, letting my finger rest on one, purple, purple, blue, yellow, purple, red, red, just a little longer
than would be considered normal, the aperture can
be detected, and will open, will desperately open,
and I will be free.

•

But instead, no, they have come with questionnaires and we are seated at a long oblong table laid
out with blotters and inkpots, folded snowy napkins, little bowls of salt, white and magenta sweet
peas in elegant crystal vaselets, rubber stamps that
say CONFIDENTIAL, and, oddly, pincers made

of teak. The questionnaire is printed on pallid, beautiful green paper, paper the color of a shiny chrysalis. "Turn pages with pincers," is clearly marked in blue ink on the front. "TURN PAGES WITH PINCERS. DO NOT USE HANDS." Answers to the questions are to be spoken into a small microphone affixed to the chair. Our legs are shackled to an upholstered ring that protrudes from beneath the carpet. The chair, unfortunately, is too low and I must strain my neck to read the questionnaire. There are one hundred and eighty items but we are given no hint as to how long we may take to answer them, an hour, four hours, twenty minutes . . . ? The pincers seem to have been oiled, or greased somehow. There are eighteen items to a page. Each is an hypothesis and we are to rate its probability of occurring as an "everyday reality." The word "everyday" is not defined or clarified. Our choices are the same for every item: (a) 100% (b) 75% (c) 50% (d) 25%, or (e) 0%. Item twenty-three: "A blue ball printed with advertising slogans rolls toward you down a sloped cobbled alley dappled with sunshine, and uniformed military officers scramble after it, screaming, 'Bomb! Bomb!'" Item forty: "Two little girls in pinafores skip rope next to a pleasantly murmuring stream while their parents eat fish sandwiches and pickles from an array of foodstuffs spread on a plaid blanket. Thunderclouds roll in from the west." By the time I am at item fifty-two, "In a Turkish Bath a slender man wrapped in a red towel offers a sealed envelope," beads of sweat are moving down my cheeks and I am urgently needing to urinate. Ushers in gold jackets pass back and forth behind our backs. Item sixty-six: "A creeping honeysuckle entraps a tarantula escaped from a pet shop in a nearby residential district." Item seventy is interesting: "Explosive missiles from a military enemy are sighted by radar at the instant the radar operator is being dressed down by a superior for overzealousness and lack of respectful demeanor." The oiled teak pincers by means of which I am attempting to turn the pages are less and less efficacious as the number of pages to turn dwindles and the final pages, long pressed under the weight of the previous ones, stick together recalcitrantly. I hear the gentleman on my left murmuring into his microphone, "50% ... 50% ... 50% ... 50%...." I wonder whether he was once a mathematician and has calculated the odds of each hypothetical situation as equivalent, since all are equally hypothetical. "50% ... 50%...." Item one hundred and fourteen:

"In a Moroccan delicatessen which normally sells twenty types of soft cheese, and on a Sunday morning, a gunman demands hostages." One of the ushers, behind my back, calls across the table to his colleague, a short man with an itchy ear, "When this is done, don't forget the Austropandiacus has to be watered." At item one-seventy-two I feel a desperate hunger for chocolate and apricots. At one-seventy-four this is replaced by a feeling of just having eaten chocolate and apricots. One-seventy-five: "You have gone fishing to a northern lake near Tibet. There are no fish today. Your boat is white. Your companion, removing a bandana, reveals hideous facial scars. You are homesick." Item one-eighty is very queer but now I can hardly breathe: "The larvae of the Nutsitsa ardanella are considered a delicacy on the island of Maqaltaba and it is also true that consuming large quantities of this delight produces a short-term memory loss. Agents of National Intelligence cultivate these insects, therefore, and the laboratory extraction of cuprous anhydrous dioxystearate from the larvae is a central feature of contemporary intelligence work." It seems everyone in the room has completed the questionnaire at the same time. The shackles are undone. We are marched back to the holding chambers. They have taken the liberty of making the beds. On each pillow is a note. "Questionnaire tomorrow, 2:00 p.m." Same procedure the next day, marching outside through the exercise yard, past the laundry with the chipped rotting wooden door that was once white, down the steep pathway that leads to the sea, into the Quonset hut with the great oblong table. The questionnaire printed on yellow today. One hundred and eighty questions, this time all about little girls and little boys. Ninety-seven, for instance: "A little boy counts to ten and bounces a ball against a wall." Ninety-eight: "A little girl eats a vanilla cream pudding." The next day the questions are printed on pink and are about mollusks, all one hundred and eighty of them. "A bivalve turns slightly blue when subjected to halogen radiation," that kind of thing. The announcement is made that the questionnaires will be given daily until further notice. The man sitting next to me continues with his (not as much irritating as infuriating) practice of replying "50%" to each and every question. The ushers begin to take liberties, they smoke, they tell jokes. After a week and a half, a very tall and emaciated man in a perfectly tailored (and considerably braided) scarlet uniform comes in and announces that the ushers will be replaced. The new ushers do not seem to speak any known language. The questionnaires become more fascinating, even as they become more tedious. The hundred and twelfth one, for instance, question eleven: "Hardly does the incendiary team mount the platform when it becomes apparent the rockets will provide far too much illumination, so Recklinghaus calls for a retreat. No one is comfortable with this." 116/177: "Beans in a tin are cooked with sausage." 123/80: "The herder plants six junipers in a row and then lays down in the long grass to sleep." 206/19: "The bath water being tepid, the Duchess steps out." The afternoon questionnaire session is now so firmly set in our daily program that we look forward to it as though it were a meal. It amazes me I can be brought to express an opinion about so many hypothetical situations distant from my imagination or experience, indeed that I can be ready to fabricate answers, even eager to do so, and that with recourse to some basis or model that has been buried in an untraceable corner of my mind I can estimate, indeed discriminate, the probabilities demanded of me. How have I been readied, even refined, to make such arcane guesses? Who has been tutoring me? When? "Two fishermen trade places in a skiff. The number of fish swimming past the keel increases by threefold as they stand to do this, and then diminishes once they have taken their seats again" (303/103). How can I be in a position to comment on this, 75%, 50%, 100%, 0%? "A man sits in a public washroom of a major hotel, having his shoes cleaned. The shoe cleaner is humming a tune made popular in the 1940s. The customer reaches into his pocket to pay and finds only hundred-dollar bills" (340/106). They begin serving refreshments during administration of the questionnaires. Tea with lemon. Trays with little sugared cookies, often Hungarian cookies sprinkled with confectioner's sugar. One day, the old man who has been sitting next to me all these months, the one who always says 50%, is no longer there. "Where is Mr. Half and Half?" I ask the nearest usher, nodding at the empty chair. He says something unintelligible. But the next day the old man is back. This time he has changed his tune. "75% . . . 50% . . . 0% . . . 0% . . . 0% . . . 75% . . . 0% . . . ." I notice he never once says 100%. The next day still, he is missing again. The fourth day, he is back, and there is a sour look on his face, and his eyes are sallow, and he seems to have tremors. "0% . . . 0% . . . 0% . . . 0% . . . 0% . . . 0% . . . 0% . . . 0% . . . 0% . . . ." The next day he is gone. The day after that, he is still gone. The following day, gone. "Where is this man?" I ask again, each day— each day more forcefully—and the usher, the same dull man, chubby with pink baby cheeks and a wisp of a goatee, and who has a badge on his lapel that reads URKO, says something unintelligible but then after several more days he comes out with it: "Gone. G-o-n-e." "Gone?" say I, incredulous. "Gone. Gone. G for Gone. D for Dead." "Dead?" "Gone, yes. Dead, yes. Gone dead. Dead gone." They suspend the questionnaires. We are kept in the holding room. I bathe. I take a cigar I have made by rolling up some of the brown leaves that are scattered on the floor of my cell, light it, take a puff, and try hard to forget the man who is gone, dead gone, gone dead, dead. Tall, white-haired, angry. White angry, tall white. Green eyes. Green eyes gone. Always pointed with a tiny little twig, he did, as though it were a baton and he were conducting Mahler. Yes, not Beethoven but Mahler. What could he have meant, "0% . . . 0% . . . 0%"? Was that resistance, or acquiescence? They bring us into an assembly room and we are addressed by the Director-General in a language I cannot begin to grasp, frequently including the phrase, "Pymina swabotl tot!" Pymina swabotl tot, indeed!, but

then I have to think, Pymina. Pymina swabotl.
Swabotl tot. He concludes, magically, in English of
a sort, but I have to tell you that by this point my
English has deteriorated to the level of squatpiss:
"And so, interestingly, this is the result of your happiness," he says, almost barking, "if you but consider that we can expand and contract, both, and thus
the inflammation is rendered smooth and at once
shapely, and really we have no recourse at all, but
there are conventions we must take into account,
that's paramount, and thus it happens to be the
case that we can celebrate our misgivings and our
beatitudes, which are quite substantial and flexible,
and we can achieve a condition in which finality is
attributable, and finality is producible, and recti-
linearity is both desirable and required, unless
there are objections which are both compatible
and coherent in context." I am beginning to think
I see.

•

Back in the cells. The guards are now naked most
of the time, it's hot and humid and it seems they
can't be bothered. It is unnecessary for them to
bear weapons, these fellows, since the electromag-

netic arrangements here are so deft and practical. In fact the senior warden is a grandmother who wears velvet skirts and smokes through a cigarette holder. She squints when she signs documents. Everyone is terrified of her, but she always has a joke for people at our level, the one about the two lovers who went into the forest. . . . Indeed, she is the soul of warmth. Because she permits it, there is plenty of horseplay among the naked guards. The horseplay keeps them satisfied and her policy is, satisfaction brings devotion. And also, don't frown at the guards. We ask each other—one of the great riddles—why the guards do not ever trouble to wear clothing, because even nakedness becomes boring, even nakedness, and everyone has a theory. Clothing costs money to clean. Uniforms can be used for hiding. We are clothed but we are behind bars, after all, and the guards are free. Some say the senior warden takes pleasure gaping at the naked guards, but on the face of it this is an unprepossessing notion because, rather consistently, the senior warden seems to have been the victim of a lobotomy. In truth, I think we are a little less likely to try to touch them in their unclothed state, touch them, dominate them, and so we keep back, and without doing anything they can hold us at bay, as a tamer does big cats. We are free to turn away or watch, as we please, when the guards wrestle, and on the radio they broadcast Big Band music, and a team of designers dressed in flaming fuchsia tunics keeps passing by trying swatches of various fabrics against the bars in late afternoon light. There is a plan to swathe the cell bars in fabric so that fewer bruises will be produced when we are held against them. The guards piss in a gutter that runs the length of the corridor, and light up cigarettes they carry in little leather pouches tied to thin belts slung over their shoulders. A cleanup team comes through on Sundays, cuts our hair, sprays down the floors with a bluish white disinfectant that smells like strawberry, gives us a change of clothing. The head boy hands out shower passes. We get a new ballpoint and a notepad and the old ballpoint and notepad are collected. Outside in the yard, where I'm allowed on Sunday afternoons, I can ride a bicycle around an oval track, but today it's raining, heavy frightening rain. There's a kid named Alfini in the last cell down to my right, he's in here for something he did with a hypodermic: a skinny kid with white hair, tall, slender. The guards took him and stripped him and threw him down in the bath and stood in a circle and pissed on him. Directly.

He didn't move a muscle, and later they found him with a smile curling his lips, and catatonic. He hasn't said a word in months. Next door to me on the left, there's an architect who's always drawing designs for cornice moldings. I remember I once had a rosewood table and I used to sit there toward sunset and carve a pear with a little wooden-handled knife and sliver off Stilton and drink Black Russian tea with evaporated milk. In here, one loses the sense of difference between tantalizing and unbearable.

•

Having begged for weeks to be provided with writing equipment, the architect has been serviced with a ream of colored paper from the print shop and a felt-tipped pen, and he has produced a manifesto of sorts, hundreds of pages, so full of gigantisms of language I needed a dictionary to make heads or tails of it. But they hid it. At any rate, no such volume is here to be offered; even the chief administrator doesn't apparently have it; and so I was left with the echo of words like eirenical to dote upon ignorantly, words like praemunire and ladrone, ephippium and tittivate. He was surely a man with a twinkle in his one good eye, the architect, one whose every comment was embellished by a sentient chuckle. He said that in the outside world he had kept a pet porcupine, a very old one with long gray quills. He said also that we would never get out of here. They took him off, with his intensely decorated pages, and some hours afterward came and cleaned out his facility, and he hasn't been heard from. Some say they have him locked up in the south wing and others think there is a distinct chance he has been promoted into the administration. My fern needs a lot more light, but I have only one tiny window.

{5}

One of the young guards who wrestles naked at night with his friend outside the cells came up to my door last night and whispered at me, "We can do anything you don't want to stop us from doing." The appetite of the naked guards to engage with one another seems bottomless.

•

Our appetites are kept tame by additives drizzled into the food before they serve it, and so it is hardly a surprise, I think, that we do not in general complain about what is fundamentally an abysm of cuisine. I doubt anyone in the kitchen actually knows anything about food preparation at all. Thursdays, I think it is—the benzyladenopines and parotroparids they pump us full of make the days blend deliciously into a pastel rainbow and Thursday is Sunday before you know it, and the music helps, too, the resonating choirs yelping "Give," "Love," "Mine," "Get," "Run"—but Thursdays they have a menu that is corn chowder of a sort, thick slices of white bread, pancakes, boiled potatoes, and then cake, a pasty off-white affair with little indecipherable seeds. All of my fluids are either oxidized or supersaturated or acidified, so that my body is become altogether a kind of pipette. My urine is colorless and copious, and a little machine on the wall with a tube and a loudspeaker insists hourly that I walk up and drink. I cut my finger on a protruding door screw and saw that my blood had darkened menacingly. When I masturbate what issues—if I can distract myself long enough to become engaged in a credible fantasy—is almost mauve in the queer light they flood into this place. I have almost no sexual appetite and looking at my pendulous organ in the mirror—a piece of polished quartz—I am frequently caught by the thought of edible meat, cold cuts, and then my eye runs up my flank to my scars and I recollect the moments when I was prodded and carried away and the power stick and everything goes black.

•

Apparently a book is being written. A man was brought into the mess and introduced as the author of a study of pleasure camps such as this one:

from the beginning this place has been referred to officially as a Pleasure Camp. A smile crept into his otherwise rather moribund features at the mention of this sacred phrase, but as I think back I find it quite impossible to state whether he was experiencing sardonic bemusement or genuine thrill at the idea of our condition being associated with happiness. Indeed, it is impossible to say, or to know, whether we ourselves view this sickening irony in pain or in witty relief. Knowledge is not knowing that you do not know. But he has a recorder and is planning, so they say, to interview each one of us, turn by turn, and make the whole thing into a very revealing, honest, and compelling book. My interview was fruitless, in my opinion, but he did express a great deal of concern spasmodically batting his twinkly blue eyes and he did wait patiently and allow for the full range of guttural silence I was able to produce in answer to his arcane and flighty questions. Quite a few of these were about my relations with other "clients," as he called the inmates, and I could reply only by saying that this one made cigarettes and sold them for items of clothing; that another told stories; that a third offered insults, and so on. He left soon enough, wishing us a rain-free summer. Now the sky is utterly yellow with heat,

the vines are lush, hummingbirds are everywhere
on the balconies, great fat cherimoyas are flowering beside the pools in which we are not permitted
to swim but which we are obliged to scrub early
in the morning for the health of the naked guards
who love to plunge before breakfast after anoint-
ing one another with redolent figgy creams. One
of them—I call him Adonis, and why not?—has
taken to chatting with me on a regular basis, occasionally covering himself with a morsel of cloth to
disguise, if this is possible, the fact that he has an
erection. Once, while I looked down at it, he said,
"You think it is you who inspires this? No. It is my
power over you. I can have you electrocuted. I can
have you gassed." He said this quite complacently,
as though ordering raisins and oranges in a market. "I can have you behind bars at any moment.
I can have you under the surgeon's knife. When I
think about what I can do, yet what I do not do, I
am stirred by my own magnanimity." He himself
looked down and flicked his organ which gawked
up at me in a stupor. "My nakedness," he went on,
"is my power. Go. Go now. Water the lawn." I had
so many chores to do in those days. The lawns
were vast, like golf courses, and they wanted the
grass clipped by hand scissor. You could roll on the

grass at twilight—well: they could roll, we were in
our cages—and it would be like velvet, and dark
and colorless in the half light. Plenty of alcohol
was poured down throats. Adonis never took his
eyes off me, always smiled, told me insidious jokes
about the other guards. But the day after the book
was published, with my interview and everyone
else's, he failed to appear, and a rumor circulated
that he had been transferred. "Transferred," a word
nobody ever deciphered for us. But then somebody said there had been a mistake, the word was
"Transposed," and other rumors started, much
more incongruous and depressing, and someone
actually said he had been beheaded and someone
else that he had been surgically castrated and a
third that he had been promoted outside the camp
altogether: it was impossible to know what to believe. But I never saw him again. And the book was
soon recalled and harshly expurgated, whole chap-
ters hacked out, and it was recirculated as a long
pamphlet with numerous titillating color illustrations showing the tropical parks, the towering rho-
dodendron gardens, the seven interlocking lakes,
the great hydrangea circle with the eleven species
of hydrangea as tall as elephants, a tennis match, a
bowl of soup all steaming and fabulous, two bright

youths in gay orange costumes chatting innocently under a jacaranda tree....

• • •

All this was written, I am told, years ago. I do not remember having inscribed any of it, nor do I recollect any of the facts or experiences these sentences relate. It was found buried behind bricks in the wall. I read it now, as do you, a stranger in strange precincts. What I have been told in the official briefings—given in a low red brick building at the University of California, San Diego—is only this, and I choose to believe it: that they found me in a deeply drugged state in the south of England in August of 1995. Beneath the castle town of Lewes, and between the villages of Rodmell and Piddinghoe, is the British Rail stop at Southease, where a curving thread of road snakes between lush mallows and crosses the sultry brown Ouse. The barriers had been left raised, putting up alarums all the way to Wimbledon, and I was upon the worn wooden surface of the bridge adjacent the station, with the skin on my back and the backs of my arms much abraded, as though by lashings. To the east, at the top of the hill leading to the A26, a boy sell-ing his teacher's honey from a little card table at the Itford Farm took an idle moment to gaze off toward the tracks and saw something in the hazy light, ran down to see better, came upon me, tried to revive me, then returned and sent his father, a stern and upright builder who carried me to his house and rang the police. Thence I was taken, first to Lewes Hospital, then to London Hammersmith, finally to a second resting place near St Pancras Station—about any of these places I cannot recollect anything but I am reliably informed—and thereafter I came down by train to a sanitarium at the edge of the woods in Grantchester Meadow, bordering Cambridge. The sanitarium is not recorded in my memories, but I can call up an image of a tea garden down the road where the requisite scones are given up under apricot trees with the requisite jam and cream, and also a charming pub with a superb muesli for breakfast if you sleep there, which I think I did, and a long field bordering a stream where there are butterflies and dragonflies and cows and tall grasses running on, it seems, forever. If you examine the files you will see that they show me staying a full three years in Grantchester, apparently reading the Aenead with some diligence, before being moved by motorcade to London Heathrow and placed, sedated upon a stretcher, on a flight to the west coast of the United States. A motel in La Jolla was my next home, only a little way down Coast Blvd. from the white clapboard cottage where I write these lines now, and I was there, apparently, four months and four days. But the decoration of my consciousness is begun with my stay here upon the cliff. The house I am in is very small, has been rented from someone I do not know, a professor of semantics on leave to Canada. There is a sunroom looking northwest, with the Beach and Tennis Club and the Scripps Institute below me to the right. Sliding down from where I sit is a thick meadow of banana yellow ice flowers peopled by curious gray squirrels and guarded by armies of brown pelicans who swoop back and forth all afternoon as the tide moves. A pathway runs along the cliff top and I walk there and try to reconstruct what can have happened to me, what world I can have inhabited, before being awakened here. The narrative you have read, if we can call it that, was supplied me a few days ago inside a large translucent pink plastic envelope, and it was with some distinct shock that I saw my own name upon the title page. Some of what is contained in it may have truth, I am forced to admit, for it does seem, in certain spots, dimly plausible to me. But I suspect most, if not all, of this story is a concoction brewed by unknown forces from some reality or quasi-reality unimaginable to me and then presented as my own diary for purposes I cannot begin to fathom. I realize that one reason the producer of this material might wish to affix my name is the simplest: that for a testament to be taken seriously as real, some author, any author, is better than none at all, and that as in the vast field of human population some author had to be discovered, I was no less likely than any man to be ultimately named to the prize. All this, given that there is a small library of titles bearing my name, and so the writer, whoever he actually is, could have had every sensible reason for believing I might swiftly be adopted as the "author." Me more likely than many, indeed, because I was incapacitated to make denial. Yet I have to say in honesty that some shards of this bear the most distinct tincture, for me, of both resonance and personality, convey to me, like ammonia spirited up the nose, a sharp and direct sensation of the actual, the fleeting, the real. The bizarre questionnaires, for example, and the old man who eventually vanished. The warden-grandmother. The lovers in the pool in the forest. One question remains to plague me. Why, indeed, should any effort have been expended—they have spared nothing, I should tell you: funds, perquisites, telephone calls in the middle of the night, testimony of witnesses—in attempting to convince me that these words are mine? As I have said, I am weak, and powerless to issue denials, and so they can make their claims at little expense, and with formidable surety, yet why do they wish to make their claims? My conviction seems more important to them than anything, and they stop at nothing to lure from my face the tears of recognition and identification. I am certainly a wreck and this fact must bring them delight, since it brings them assistance. I am left, at any rate, if without much of a mental past, at least with their packet of files to bolster my voyage into the future. I can consult the pages. I have been consulting just a little, and already it is true that, reading certain passages over and over, I slide into a curious transport of comfort and acceptance, as though I can imagine myself having penned this painful scrawl in some darkened recess, secretly, at night, over many years, and in a trance of fear and relenting. I have made the unthinkable step, indeed (because ultimately it is the method which most irreproachably relieves the

pain of wonder), of coming to think, "Possibly." O,
a word like poison or pearls. "Possibly, in the fur-
thest reach of the imagination, given certain circumstances. . . ." The more I read, the narrower becomes the gap between what I suspect and believe
myself to be and to have been and what the text
implies, and the richer (as closer) grows the bond
between myself as reader of these passages now and
my possible self as creator of the same things then.
Then, the key word. *Then*, and the thousand thousand thousand *thens*. And more, it is true that I
fear—yet hungrily look forward to—the moment
when I will utterly accept the bizarre dream of
these pages and by accepting dissipate it, so that it
is dream no more. I feel sure the time is approaching. One day I will proclaim this text, knowing, yet
also averring, that this is my story, that I am the
man who was in that place, behind those bars, that
I was put there for a reason not yet explicated
and—in a tortuous ceremony of investigation, sup-
position, and doubt—yet to be discerned; that
these images, haunting my imagination, are in
truth drawn up from the facts of my life. I will be a
hesitant convert, to be sure. I will acknowledge
having written this, but out of my crazed, my
drugged, imagination. But then, I both suspect

and dread, I will come to know, in one of those flashes of inspiration that leave no prints and exert no pressure, that there were no drugs at all, that there was no craziness. I will see that it happened, in plain fact: every nuance. It will be clear that my life and my dream not only exist as interchangeable domains but must be, in the light of truth, interchangeable and interchanged. What I have been thinking myself to be living now and what I held true for myself before the capture: these are the fantasy. And what I had thought a fantasy, someone's fantasy, someone's idea of my fantasy, or indeed mine and only mine, is my life. Perhaps it is only a matter of hours before I step to that conclusion. It is now Friday, a beautiful sunny day, and the surf is pounding. Pelicans are soaring past my window. I will walk down the cliff path to the shell shop, grab a piece of carrot cake and cup of tea at the Goldfish Point Café (pausing for a piss, perhaps, in the largest restaurant washroom west of the Rockies), make my way by Coast Blvd. to the tide pools where the seals and the dolphins swim together with the Garibaldi fish in the sparkling inky blue sea, the moss on the flat rocks threatening me excitingly as I navigate it barefoot to get close to the water. I will be able to tell myself that if

ever I was in a prison, today I am free. I will watch
the seals and the seals, with inscrutable friendship,
will watch me. But in order to know that freedom,
will I not have to acknowledge that imprisonment,
the text of that imprisonment, as a prelude? If I
re-enter that old text, now newly as its maker, is it
not true that I will have to doubt this shoreline a
little, this salt smell, these flying birds, these foam
caps, the roar of this ocean upon these stones, this
brazen sun, all this *reality*? Will I not be forced to
wonder if they are as real as I suppose, these little
flowers, and if I can touch them—if, indeed, I am
here touching them, because I do believe I am here,
with the Café just ahead, across the tiny sloping
street, and the pelicans cawing—or if once again,
and without the slightest warning, and with the
bridge of memory in ruins, I have awakened to
only a story that I must struggle to accept as my
own, a text that is being attributed to me but that I
have, in truth, only newly found and not yet put
into my own poor words. Already in the cataclysm
produced by these doubts, the cliff path is breaking
apart under my feet (a frog has quickly crossed before me into the pale ice plants) and the turquoise
sea divides. The path is narrowing. A fragment of
the cliff is juxtaposed now against a fragment of

the sky, all fragments! A fragment of the tide pools—half a mile away, but what is a mile?—is abutted to the shell shop, here, on my left, toward which I step but which I cannot reach. I am both here and there at once, and it is both then and now. But already I am somewhere else concocting this, surrounded by soothing richly painted walls. I cannot see outside, and do not know the name of this city. Children sing *Adeste fidelis*, and why not? There is an array of ferns in a long window. A baseball deal is being reported somewhere on a television. A plane flies high overhead in the blue black silence, heading, perhaps, north.

Dream Sonata

ANDANTE PACIFICO

A motorboat passed swiftly beside the cliff. White-caps to the horizon. Along the pathway looking down upon the water were blankets of ice plants, yellow and purple, covering red rock. Behind one's back, past the houses at the top of the rise and down the street in front of the houses, in a little theater, people watched something by Jean Renoir and went out to little cafés and, sitting, discussed characters and story. *Diary of a Chambermaid.* Outrage, shame, disrespect, hideous pain, shame, embarrassment, pride, the fulsomeness of lust, the shame of lust, retreat, pride, hauteur, shameful hauteur, dignity eclipsed by shameful hauteur, penetrating eyes, a bitter pair of lips, fingers, eclipse, fingernails, thighs, pathways, tombs, stones, a motorboat passing. Two men are in the motorboat. "Rectangles," calls one—it's unmistakable. The other seems to cry, "You're the richest man on the coast. Christ, you're rich. I'm sick of how rich you are, I can't stand it." The first one says again, "Rectangles." Overhead now are pelicans the color of bleached farm fences. Up in the village past the houses at the top of the rise, down the street, in the restaurants, in one particular restaurant, at one table in the restaurant, under lamps that bring heat in the cool spring, eating rillettes of pork, drinking Mouton-Cadet, discussing Bernanos, Renoir, Du Bouillet, Rambutan, Narcisso Yepes, Vincius de Moraes, Jobim, Diegues, Tolucca, Borges, Montoya, Don Carlos de Quivinha, Revueltas, *The Band Wagon*, Pascale Rogé, Alicia de Larrocha, Chico Buarque, Hindemith, Jane Grigson, Helena Rubenstein, Stokowski, platform heels, the stars as they appeared in the sky over Rio de Janeiro on 15 November, 1889, semolina pudding, the history of condenser microphones, Sarah Vaughn, Phil Rizzuto, Norman Panama, the Panama Canal, Norman Dello Joio, Vincent Van Gogh painting in Saint Rémy de Provence, frog legs, hilltops especially in Sussex, the Musée des Beaux Arts in Valparaiso, Die Kunstmuseum in Basle, Die Architektonen Schaftenhausenschift von der Nachlass im Bildernstreigen, the last words of Archibald Newbury, the types of illumination used in parking lots (especially sodium vapor), the pier at Santa Monica on Wednesday nights in March, the Venice Beach at 9:30 p.m. on Sundays in October, monads, cognac-colored velvet, Proust in red bindings (cherry red), reindeer, Jobim, Stanislas Skoracewski, ranunculus fields near San Diego, Norman Mailer's *The Armies of the Night*, snow, lying down at night under moonlight in soft fields of snow, deer by moonlight, chopped pistachio nuts, semolina pudding, La Musée de faience de Strasbourg, the long road to Geneva winding upward in the Jura, the long road to Anaheim, the orange trees of Anaheim, the fences encircling the orange trees, the lemon trees on the lawns, the orange trees on the lawns of Nice, the orange trees in the park, the park in darkness, the silent purple darkness swelling the park, Vinicius de Moraes, she leans across the table to him imagining they are in darkness in a whirlpool looking up at the stars surrounded by coconut palms naked Jobim singing with a drowning voice the moon filtered purple the motorboats throbbing the waiter bringing the bill, mints, ink, gasoline, lacquer, vermilion, trumpet vines, a hummingbird, The Coca Cola Bottling Company of Nashville Tennessee, the flat, very flat pebbles of the quarry of Santo Emilio, the green barn, Mars bars, jade, garlic, plastic, bromine, real calculus, nasturtium blossoms, carbonic acid, keychains, a letter from the Director of the School for Advanced Placement in International Relations

(London), the hot sweet summer smell of sizzling shrimp, a mule, the entry in the *Dictionary of the American Language* under "reticent," the rivers of Alberta in alphabetical order, the Von Karajan performance of *Fidelio*, the father of Perugia, the hills of Rome, the hills of Jerusalem, the hills of Los Angeles, the hills of Anacapri, up into the hills, the ranunculus wild in the hills, Vinicius de Moraes, Betty Furness, fluorescent lightbulbs, naugahyde, arborite, sconces, glass-topped tables, gilded frames, Jussi Bjørling, manuscripts tied with string, purple liquid and blue tiles, a letter from Fred P., a dead rose, dead roses tied in a bundle, pot-pourri of dead roses in a wooden bowl, Chico Buarque, a cheque stub from the Café Europa on East 54th Street, Manhattan, escalators, green lights, Massimo Corti, the S. S. Nederhallen, flights of angels sing thee to thy rest, these fragments I have shored against my ruins, full fathom five thy father lies, everything had the look of something that is looked at, no man is an island, on the wall was a picture that, never having been to Rome, he thought was Rome but that everyone who had been to Venice knew was Venice, or something very like that, very like, most like, something most like, most seemly, unseemly and seemly at once, posting with such

dexterity to incestuous sheets, she leans across
the table, everything of him can be smelled by her
in the warm drafts of air produced by the candle
flame, the sea, swimming, the motorboat in the
sea, the pelicans, "rectangles," "You're ridiculously
rich," "I can't stop," "The richest man alive," the pelicans in flight, the pelicans swooping, and she leans
across the table, the waiter brings the bill, the waiter moistens his fingers for the candle, the moss-fla-
vored candle, she stands, Vinicius de Moraes, the
night is purple, the pelicans swoop, he stands with
her, Gongora, they walk near one another, Gongora, Vinicius de Moraes, her hand wishes to be sliding down his back, the waiter has the bill, Gongora,
Vinicius de Moraes, Alfred Nobel, he has entered
her reserve, he is in her forest, he is being chased
by her gameskeeper, the stag is afoot, Gongora, the
stag has fled, the stag is bled, Gongora, Gongora,
Vinicius de Moraes, Alfred Lord Tennyson, Chico
Buarque, *Tess of the D'Urbervilles*, reading glasses
with polished quartz lenses, polished quartz lenses,
polyquat linden, polyglot Linzmen, canoe drawn
onto the island, charcoal, "NO TRESPASSING,"
his arrow flying toward the stag across the brook,
his arrow flies, he arches back, she breathes for
him, does he breathe?, she breathes for him, she

cannot run, the brook is frozen over, she breathes for him, she breathes for him, Chico Buarque, O, O, on the night of 15 November 1889, above Rio de Janeiro, the stars.

PRESTISSIMO

And now, and now that we have dispensed with
this prolegomenon, and now that these introduc-
tory requirements have been met, and the stage is
set, and the passageways are open to certain configurations, and the patterns are imprinted, and now
that the animals are fed and ready, and now that the
fish are in the tanks, and now that the trained seals
which are in truth trained sea lions because—look
at those front fins—and now that the menus have
been arrayed on the sideboards, and at this time,
in these precious few moments, with these threads,
with this scepter, and now with this scepter, and
now when you are anticipating the movement of
the scepter into the swath of diamonds, and now
as the stars are like diamonds, and now ladies and
gentlemen, and now children of all ages, and now
that the arguments have been framed and put
forth, and now that the moorings have been cast
off, and now that the bindings have been loosed,
that the shoes have been arranged on the tree, that
the tree has been decorated, that the decorations
have been itemized in the account books, that the

future has been predicted, that the stars have been mapped, that the buses have been delayed, that the water wafers have been set in rows upon the platters of herring, and now that we have fished, and now that we have been victorious, and now that we know, it is imperative, truthfully, without the least guarantee, for certain reasons, and for certain as far as certainty can be calculated, that, and always, here, for you, because you are who you are and I am who I am, because we eat together, because the pelicans fly, the boat capsized, the flags, the nuptial flags, the deck, the chairs in lines, the uniforms bright, the sunlight, the glazing sun, the deck, the chairs in the blazing sun, the white uniforms, the blue sky, the caps, the uniforms, and now that we cannot see, and now that we hope, for you, for you and all that you wish to be, because I am I and you are you, I send to you, only you, I send off briquets, then a flame, then what can be done in a flame, I am and you are, you are who you are, then the decoration, then the caps up in the blue sky, then the pelicans flying and the paint-by-numbers boxes, and the starch that makes us tremble, I send you, now that you are there, that you may be at ease, the flag, all the flags, to mount in the east, I send, trembling, pelicans flying, a flag, the blazing sun, my flag, our flag, my flag that I offer as our flag, a flag supreme, a word.

But that is not enough.

We suffer.

We do not comprehend.

But we are ready to comprehend.

The stage is set. The dossier is open. The pencils are lifted. We sit. The flag flies. We look up. The pelicans swoop. A knock comes at the door. We do not answer, ready to understand, having been briefed, knowing what to expect, having few anticipations that cannot be satisfied, remembering little, planting the codes. And now I must tell you, you must grasp this, that there has been a signal. A signal has been sent. Well: perhaps not exactly a signal. An artifact has been illuminated in such a way that it can be read as a signal, in such a way that those who scan the territory for information may make claims. And now I am obliged, but also pleased, to admit that I have read a signal, I have been informed, we have climbed the tower so the challenge of the tower is past us, we have gone straight to the top.

I must tell you we have gone straight to the top, the tower is past, this is not what I had imagined it would be, this liquid in this glass is not champagne, these people we have been watching are not lovers, this antagonism in the darkness has been less than an argument, the expectation was only a surfeit, the breads are cooling.

GAVOTTE

There has been, at any rate, an envelope. The handwriting both obscure and familiar. The scent both exotic and familiar. Delivered by hand. A card inside. A great many formulae, crabbed tiny writing, lavender ink. We've put them through every section and nobody can make sense of it. The Brigadier's officer insists upon recourse to metalinguistics, emails start arriving from halfway around the country urgently suggesting we take the central message to be the existence of the card itself. Paper analysis, fibrochemistry, luminoptics, splasinoscopy. "They didn't have to contact us but they did anyway," that sort of thing. Much attention paid to the timing of the arrival in relation to the secret negotiations in California and the clandestine meeting that was held yesterday morning on the seventeenth floor here. Fallenby's people. Reinaldo himself flown up from Caracas (hates flying). He comes in with sunglasses and tight lips and goes into Dieterle's briefing room with the plate glass wall. Tea served and Reinaldo not taking any. Lots of people writing furiously—every word he says.

The sense that our department has been singled out. La Venturro summoned from the art department with a set of colored gels. The curtains dropped. Everyone convinced a call will be put through to the Ministry of Defence, and indeed, from eleven o'clock until half past noon the switchboard is completely tied up. I can't get confirmation of a dental appointment, the phones are so loaded. Reinaldo's two assistants—we call them Bibsy and Bobsy—make themselves at home in my office, pull the blinds, start projecting slides with aerial views of farms onto my western wall, from which they have taken down a nice reproduction Balthus. The place is suffused with a tension and also a childlike sweetness—we're all in this together, we're family, the old strain. We're all chums. I've liked you since the day I met you. Rather like a gavotte. Reinaldo's press people prepare a statement which our own press people go over four or five times while cramming crab sandwiches into themselves and slurping Pellegrino, and then the press people give it to the legal people and the legal people give it to the spin guy, who has just arrived from New York and been dropped on the roof by helicopter; and the spin guy sends it all back for re-writing. It goes around for an hour or so and my secretary, a gaunt Maori named Helen Te Handa, faxes it to the Times. Reinaldo's gang, the spin guy, some dullards from security all vanish up to the roof. The phones start ringing. The local police show up and start dusting the envelope for prints. The head of the legal office sends one of his flunkies down to inform us we are to give no further statements. Wolfman, who received the envelope in the first place, has no intention of giving it up, and has slipped it between some leaves of pink tissue paper into the inside pocket of his jacket. It's getting late, it's five-thirty, it's dark, and it's beginning to snow. Heavy, relentless snow, that could go on like this all night. No one wants to let Wolfman go home with the envelope, they want him to lock it in the safe, two security guys are going over him in his office, rapping their fingers impatiently on his desk. He keeps saying he wants to go home to his wife and kids, and the envelope came to him— him and nobody else—and nobody has to panic, he'll guard it with his life, with his absolute life. They keep saying, "No one's talking about panic," but they won't let him out of his office. Now it's seven o'clock. In the boardroom they've got the news on and, of course, there's no mention of this, not a syllable. Wolfman is pacing around in his shirtsleeves, getting red and raising his voice. One of the security guys, in a chartreuse shirt with a red tie, comes out and makes a phone call. Soon they're announcing they have Wolfman's wife and kids in a limo in the parking lot downstairs and they're going to bring them up. Calls to security to arrange all this. "You don't goddam bring them here!" cries Wolfman, but nobody's listening. Our legal guys are back, making sure they don't look into anybody's eyes, and Molero's personal secretary all the way from the twenty-second floor, just sitting around being very demure in her navy business suit and babbling on a white cell phone in Parisian French, "Non non, c'est épouvantable!," and they have Wolfman in the briefing room now with a carafe of coffee and a quiche that he won't eat. His family is with him, the kids watching old episodes of "The Simpsons" and the wife looking petrified and white, white as lilies, a plump woman with lines under her eyes and small fingers. Apparently somebody's on his way from the Office of the National Security Advisor in Washington—plane's in the air. Wolfman is saying, "This is mine. If I put it in the safe, I know I'll never see it again." He's not crazy. My secretary is making tea for everybody, and also running around with a miniature tape recorder trying to get people to make statements she can type up. And now there's a call from the Government guy in his aircraft, for Molero's secretary, and she spends a long time repeating something and writing it down, "Valleyfield. Folley vealed? Folly? Volley?" She hangs up and calls upstairs and goes over the whole thing three times with Molero, and comes back and informs us that we have to have the card gone over by another cryptography team, this one from the Sperling Institute at Harvard, the big boys. So the phones are going crazy for another hour and we get the assurance they're on the way. Apparently they have an algorithm. Everybody is whispering "Algorithm," as though it's an aphrodisiac. Meanwhile, the Government guy shows up, asks a lot of inane questions—"What time did the envelope arrive, precisely? And I mean precisely."—looks at Wolfman through the plate glass wall of the briefing room, goes into Dieterle's private office and starts snoozing on the Mies van der Rohe sofa. We're told the Harvard guys are coming by car. Somebody sends out for cold drinks. And it's about this time that Wolfman's wife snaps, pulls a gun out of her handbag, and starts firing at our security guys through the plate glass wall of the briefing room. The kids are still watching TV. Wolfman is throwing his hands up in hysteria, and standing on a chair yelling, "You see! You see!" The wife has plugged one of the security guys in the thigh, blood spurting against yellow-and-white Pierre Frey laid on Dieterle's corridor walls at a cost of thirteen thousand dollars. The guy has collapsed to his knees and has a look of anguish on his blue face, and his eyes are glazed. She's moving around and has popped the other security guy in the shoulder and he's whining like a stuck pig. "Outa here!" she's screaming to Wolfman and she's got him wrapped in one arm. Molero's secretary has her jaw frozen open. "Take it, take it!" Wolfman screams at me and throws the envelope in my direction. The kids come running and stomp all over it as they stampede out the doors with their parents. The four of them take the fire stairs. "Jesus, I'm bleedin' to death!" says the security guy who got it in the shoulder, and he's flopped back in a great spreading red lake now. Two of the legal guys are trying to apply pressure to his arm. The envelope is now a little blood speckled. I go to the bar and pour myself a huge Laphroaig. Molero's secretary is back on the phone, walking away from me as fast as she can and burying herself in the women's lav. I go back into my office and lock the door, put myself behind the desk on the floor with my head near an open window. There's moonlight enough to read by. I see that the envelope has cards printed in dark lettering in formulae I can't make out. My phone buzzes. There's a soft knock at my door. I get up. I wait. I open the door. It's the guy from the Office of the National Security Advisor, tall, muscular, not so young, in a dark suit, with one of those faces you forget even while you're looking at it. "I come in?" I back away and pick up my phone. It's Molero's secretary, whispering, "Say nothing. Do nothing. Say nothing!" The National Security guy is sitting on the edge of my desk, opening his fat thigh a little. "This is one zoo," says he, "one fucking zoo." He asks for a Laphroaig, too. We sit together sipping, not saying a word. "What concerns me," he says finally, very tired, not really concerned, a voice that's as green as chlorophyll, "is the possibility that this communication may have no meaning at all. Because in that case, I'd have to assume it's a decoy for something else we haven't found yet. That situation you wouldn't like." This possibility, I will admit, hasn't struck me at all, but I can see right away he's no fool and I'm suddenly glad he's sharing my drink. "They've got half the brains in the country focused on your office right now," he goes on, "and maybe it's all for nothing. And I mean, of course, absolutely nothing." He says the word "absolutely" as though tasting Beluga. I hand him the envelope. He smiles. I smile back. We pour two more Laphroaigs. "Too bad you haven't got any smoked salmon," says he. He turns on my desk lamp—it's Danish—and spreads the envelope smoothly on my blotter. He pulls a little metallic pen knife from his pocket and from the side of it extracts a tiny centimeter rule. (Government jet, I tell myself. No weapons inspection.) He measures the envelope. From a pocket he withdraws, and pops into his eye, a jeweler's loupe. He slowly withdraws the three cards, lays them side by side, and bends over them, carefully humming Bill Evans's "Waltz for Debby," and then Richard Rodgers and Lorenz Hart's "Bewitched, Bothered and Bewildered." I take advantage of the moment to wish I'd arranged for a sofa in my office, then stretch myself out on the carpet while he works. "It's certainly no known language," he says quietly. "Do you mind if I photograph these?" I tell him I couldn't care less what he does, which is the truth, because he's so amicable and so very polite, and it's also true he's become my only friend, for whom I have the warmest regard, and I'm happy for him to make himself happy doing absolutely anything. But Helen's at the door now, to say the professors from Harvard are here. The Government guy looks up a little nervously, then hands her the envelope and the cards—but not before quickly shooting them with a cute little Canon Elf-5600. She disappears with the stuff leaving a cloud of Jo Malone honeysuckle and ginger behind her. We go out. Ambulance attendants are in process of stretchering and wheeling out the two security guys, and one of the legal guys has taken a bullet across the outer surface of his wrist and is being bandaged by a paramedic who speaks with a lisp. The Harvard people disappear into Dieterle's office. Now it's ten-thirty. Somebody starts asking about Molero's secretary but nobody can find her anywhere. Helen goes home. The legal guys are loafing around conversing in a language that's plain English but I don't understand, and invoking Dieterle and Molero and Reinaldo. "What is that guy from Washington?" one of them says suddenly, and they all start looking around and muttering "Jesus!", but it turns out my buddy has also disappeared into the sunset. Just some melting ice cubes in a glass are all that's left. "Is somebody going to tell Dieterle about all of this?" says one of the legal guys, "Is somebody going to phone Dieterle in Rome?" Two of the legal guys go off with two of our assistants to debate whether or not Dieterle should be phoned. Meanwhile, the Harvard team is making noise in Dieterle's office, then lulling, then yelling again, then one of them is making a speech. Through the thick door none of it is clear, but there is little doubt they are having a hard time. Code stripping, it turns out, is virtually impossible unless the straight crypto guys, who are all computer folk, manage right off the bat to get it. That's because if the basic transformations don't apply, there are no particular probabilities of any other ones fitting, and you just have to pick a needle out of the haystack. Except that in the case of codes—which is to say, systems of readable signs—the haystack is roughly the size of Europe and the needle is roughly the size of a proton. At the beginning you just have to take a guess, and there are too many possible guesses, equally possible because equally hopeless. "Why . . . ," they've decided to conduct a little interview and they have me in a chair facing a pair of glaring lights, "Why do you suppose a message would be sent to this particular office? To you?" I tell them that actually it was crazy Wolfman who got it. Then one of our assistants barges in to report that the police have put out a bulletin on Wolfman's wife, and that none of the Wolfman family got home. "But," they want to know, "was it aimed at Mr. Wolfman? It would help if we could assume it was designed for him." I couldn't help them, because we just rotate doing the mail, sorting it, and today it was Wolfman's day. "Could the sender have known this?" A preposterous question, since on one hand anybody can know anything and on another nobody can know anything, but they're desperate, we're desperate, everybody's getting desperate. We interrupt our regular mail rotation all the time, it was just that today we didn't, I tell them. Wolfman's paralegal runs in with the news that Mrs. Wolfman has surrendered, down near the river in a spaghetti joint called Emilio's. They are taking her in for a psychiatric examination. The Harvard people admit it could take years to break this code, if indeed it is a code, if indeed it is a message. The legal guys have no interest in considering the possibility that this is not a coded message. They are already scribbling protocols for chains of command and public release schedules. It's almost gone midnight. Somebody calls from Accounting to ask whether the social security numbers are available for the men from Harvard, for the two wounded security guys (hired on for the day, it seems), and for Wolfman (who, inexplicably, isn't in the system). I'm hoping I can go home and get such a good night's sleep that when I wake up in the morning all this will have been a dream. I tell the Harvard team the envelope was registered by Wolfman and turned over by him to me; and so, according to Departmental regulations, I am responsible for it and I am authorized to keep it in my possession. Sometimes you lie without even realizing it. Each of the three of them looks at me as though I'm crashing a party. Grudgingly they hand it over and I wrap it in plastic and stick it in my briefcase and head home. A police cruiser is tailing me all the way to the park. There's a message from Helen on my tape at home, to the effect that the two wounded security guys will live and that Wolfman has been suspended—big surprise. I lie in the darkness for an hour, listening to the traffic swooping by and thinking about Wolfman and how we met one day fishing for a key to the supply room. He'd never shown me a moment's kindness or amiability before that. I'd always thought his wires were pulled a little tight. He was the kind of guy who doesn't say hello in an elevator. It occurs to me that the formulae on the cards may have been written in fading ink. I jump out of bed, take the envelope from my jacket and stow it in the freezer, between Ben & Jerry's Cherry Garcia and some waffles. Something tells me there's more to Wolfman's wife going nuts than met the eye. He had a funny look when the guy from Washington showed up. For one instant, I saw him look up in that briefing room, stare through the plate glass wall into the tall man's face, and a flicker of something passed through his eyes: not fear, not quite knowledge or recognition. The flicker of the intelligence as it scans a universe of records for a single entry it knows it will find. Sleep is now looming up in a thick wave and rather too quickly, though now I don't want it. I suspect that in the morning my freezer will be empty. I hear Bill Evans playing his dead piano.

Andante cantabile

Near Saintes Maries-de-la-mer. The old lady was
dying, and so word had been sent to the doctor to
come. Out in the marshes the doctor was riding
the bulls in, since this was a Tuesday and on Tues-
days he rode with the other men of the Étang.
Monstrous blackbirds made vortices in the sky
above, and he spotted one against a white cloud
and watched it head west, east, west, east again, in
a vitiating spiral of indecision. His pinto splashed
through the shallow marsh decisively and he told
himself how it would be well to secure a position
for himself in a city up north, and so get out of
here. The boy came running along the pathway
waving the note in the air. "Quickly, you must
come quickly, my grandmother . . . !" And then, as
if for emphasis, "Monsieur le médecin! Monsieur
le médecin!" The sun dropped like a steamed apricot into the green rice paddies. The old lady's fever
was spiking and her pulse was virtually non-exis-
tent, only the shadow of the shadow of a drumbeat.
She pulled him close to her, brought her lips near
his ear. "I have a secret." The words came out of her

mouth like dry papers. "Rest, Madame. . . ." Her eyes had blue fire, she sneered, she pulled him down again. "I want to tell you that my husband, you know who I mean, Gévigne—" She pushed him away and looked into his eyes coldly. He was a very young man, too young to have known Gévigne, and some wind had jiggled the structure of her mind so that she knew it. "My husband was a killer." He saw her hands trembling upon his sleeves as she caught at him to hold her aloft in the dark sea which was swallowing her. "Gévigne killed the . . . the . . ." The doctor put a cool cloth on her forehead and, turning his head, asked that water be boiled. "Water?" said the grandson, "From the marsh or fresh from the stream?" The doctor said it didn't matter. He needed to sterilize the cloths that would be bandages. Antibiotics might help, nothing else would; he injected her. Her skin was gray. She fell into sleep. The boy returned with a pail and put water on the fire to boil. The doctor soaked pieces of an old shirt he had taken from the old lady's chest and quartered with his knife. "She is your mother's mother, or your father's mother?" he asked the boy. The kid had a way of pursing his lips when he thought. "This one is not really my grandmother," he replied. "I call her grandmother. She is an old lady, it seems an appropriate name for her. She has no children, this one. She never had children, I believe. Well, it stands to reason. She never married." The doctor regarded the swarthy boy who now took a stick to the cotton pieces puckering in the water over the fire. "I will make you rice with langoustines," the kid said. "I am a good cook. That is why she keeps me around." The doctor sat in a big overstuffed old chair in the darkest corner of the room, watching the fire shadows flickering over the old lady's bed and thinking it would be good to get out of this place. If he could settle outside Paris, in Meudon or Asnières or even Auvers, he could lead a life that would be tranquil yet richly civilized. Here it was all vast space, and the density of human impression was replaced by gray absences. Bulls, birds, little white birds who resided on the bulls, the marsh, tiny cottages, flickering fire shadows. Life was reflection, but not substance. In the north, life would be substance. The boy came back with the rice and pink shrimps, boiled and glassy-eyed. "Have you ever heard of a man called Gévigne?" asked the doctor. The boy pursed his lips. "Gévigne? There's never been anybody named Gévigne around here. What was he, a traveler? Gévigne, that's not a Provençal name." The boy took the bandages from the boiling water with his stick, held them a few moments until they cooled enough to touch, pressed them together quickly to wring out the water, and laid them on the old lady's neck, where the gash from the bull had sliced nearly to the jugular and white bubbles were like pearls decorating the opening of the skin. Then he went out to bathe. The doctor sat with his dinner, hardly touching it, and drifted into sleep, lulled by the old lady's snoring. When he awoke, the fire was cooled and the room was pitch black, and silent. He moved the dinner plate from his lap, laid it on the floor, stood, lit a lamp, came near the bed. She wasn't moving and her lips were sealed. He came close, putting his ear near her lips. There was no sound. But suddenly, as he rose, she moaned and sat up with her eyes bright. "You have cured me, my dear," she fussed with herself. "The pain is gone entirely. I feel I will live." He brought the lamp close, sat at her side, lifted her frail hand in his. Her pulse had strengthened. Maybe she would live. He would be able to tell in the morning. "Will you take something to eat, Madame?" "Du riz," she said coldly. "Du riz au lait." The boy had not come back. He went into the front room and saw that on the stovetop a pot with rice still sat from his own dinner. There was milk in a little icebox hiding behind a woodpile covered with a carpet, and he boiled some with sugar and poured it over the rice for her. He fed her. She didn't eat much. She lay back and fell immediately into sleep. He walked out into the darkness and looked up at the dark sky. Everything here was form or smell, since there were no human relations. The looming dark cottage, with vines crawling over its roof, against a cloud shot with purple moonlight. The smell of nicotiana, and of the sea salt. He went inside again. The sour smell of the old lady. The traces of sugar and milk on the air. The charcoal smell of the fireplace in her room. He relit the fire, let it build up and die a little until it gave off an even heat. She turned in the bed. He slept and woke several times, never quite sleeping deeply or waking entirely. Once he thought she was standing beside his chair, reaching out to him, but he drifted back into sleep and opened his eyes and she was not there, and he slept, and she rolled in the bed, there was the smell of the burning wood gone cold, and he heard birds and it was morning. He went outside before looking at the old lady. He went down to the garden behind the cottage, past the bushes of thyme, and knelt at the border of the marsh to wash himself awake. When he came back, the boy was already there, making tea. "So, she's as good as new," he said, without emotion. The old lady was not in her bed, but in a minute she came round the side of the cottage and walked in the front door. "I am myself," she announced. "Did I tell you anything in my fever? I was dreaming of my son. Gévigne, my husband, is gone, a long time. But my son is also Gévigne. He went off, too. Who knows where. I don't know where. He is with a girl. Maybe he is not with a girl. He's old enough to know where to be. When I see his face, it is the face from years ago." She did not seem at all happy, though her color was back and she stood upright. "I will not trouble you, then, to be hospitable to me any longer," said the doctor, gathering his things, "If you need me again, you can send, as before. I will be south of Paris. It doesn't take very long to come down." The old lady stood like a tree, very firmly established in her place and without response. "And what you told me last night," he added, "your secret. It will remain secret with me. About the killing." For a long time she stared at him, piercingly. "The killing? What killing? Yves, more firewood," and the boy looked up and went out. "What secret are you talking of, monsieur? Killing whom? What?" The doctor felt, suddenly, utterly a fool, and indeed his tongue and lips grew thick. "You mentioned to me your husband, Gévigne, who . . ." He had placed a finger to his face. "Though now it occurs to me it could have been your son." Still she was staring at him, seeing right through him. "Come," she led him outside, blinding sunlight and rosebushes in every direction, and sea pines. "You say I spoke with you last night? No memory." He told her what she had said, word for word, and she listened hard, bending his way, and looked at him like a judge. Then a little laugh came out, a choking laugh. "I say things, you know. It doesn't mean anything. Last night I was probably delirious. I have that, and not so infrequently. But even when there's no delirium, I say things." The doctor wished urgently to back away, to turn, to head up the road toward Pioch-Badet, but she had his hand tightly in hers. "Do you know, have you learned in your travels, what an old lady is?" He thought if he did not free his hand he would never escape this place, never go north, never find another life, but also if he did not free his hand, just yet, she would be at peace. It wasn't that she held him in a grip. Her hand was cool and fine, like porcelain. A great fat blackbird flew overhead, cawing belligerently. She had begun to laugh, with her eyes closed, and could not stop. "You know, you have . . . given me back my . . . youth!" The doctor lunched at Pioch-Badet, there's good soup there, and stayed the night at Albaron, at a rancher's, and in the following day he took a train from Arles northward. As long as he could see the river to the west, an orange ribbon flecked with blue, the old lady stood like an implantation in his mind, laughing, her eyes river-colored, and indeed he seemed to see the years peel away from her like soft long gray leaves and her face become radiant like a planet or like a wild deer lit by a bonfire. Soon enough, however, Avignon was far behind, and then Lyon, and as the river was gone from view so was her face. He stared ahead at his future: the red velvet cushioning of the seat opposite, in the otherwise empty, dimming compartment.

Préludes (à la manière de Chopin)
to Dreams Over the Shoulder in
the Classroom When It's Raining
on a Thursday Afternoon

She stood on the tram that rattled through the night, holding the hand strap she had made her own. She looked off. She could picture the headline, "More money is not the answer." His face was flushed. He stared at her. I could see a tiny vessel throbbing in his temple. She looked off. If it were not for the concluding hurly-burly one could rest content. I thought he was rather a handsome fellow, was I misled? "It's easy. It's so easy. I can't believe how easy it is," said the ballerinas hauling in the bundles of artemisia but referring to a routine in *Coppelia*. I was always the man in a black top hat. Ever since then the tide has turned. "How will you go, or will you go at all?" Ximena Flaviana Marquesa inquired bravely. "How will you go? Will you go? How? Or will you go at all?" I was always the man in a black top hat. A kettle steamed upon the hob. "It's easy. It's so easy." A kettle I brought them from Malaysia steamed upon the hob. More money not the answer stop. Kettle steamed stop. Docking Macao Thursday. Regards Blaisdell.

(She Stood on the Tram)

They will be led, swiftly, by the cruelest path, she explained in essence, or she certainly said something like that, because we put it in the record and operations were begun and people expected them to be led and they were led. "How will you go, or will you go at all?" Ximena Flaviana Marquesa inquired caustically. "How will you go, or will you go at all?" The musician playing the viol chuckled. His face was flushed, and I could see a tiny blood vessel throbbing in his temple. She ran a hand over the soft leather of her pocketbook, thinking of the odd trinkets she had dropped into it. He stared at her. For his part, he was as otherworldly as ever, switching styles from transmuted alien promenades to his trademark drone striations. I was always the man in a black top hat. Vincent left his window sill and went back through the bedrooms to the kitchen. "I heard from them," said Ettua, "They expressed themselves." More money is not the answer. Vincent left and went back. Vincent left, went back, left, went back, left, went back, left, went back. Departing Addis Ababa early morning stop. Regards

Stavros. I was always the man. He was otherworld-ly. She thought of trinkets. More money is not the answer. His face was flushed. "It's easy. It's so easy. I can't believe how easy it is," said the buffoons, rig-ging the ropes. The musician chuckled, playing the viol and watching her. "How will you go?" Xime-na Flaviana Marquesa was persisting. "In fact, will you go at all? *Why* will you go?" Vincent left his window sill. Ever since then the tide has turned. She ran a hand over the soft leather of her pocket-book, a calloused hand, over the sweet red leather. Papers were placed in special order in separate piles under little signs on pink paper, "Bands," "Denom-inations," "Rushes," "Jackets," "Grapes," "Notwith-standing," "Tests." For his part, he was as other-worldly as ever, switching styles. I was always the man. Yellow flowers grew like tigers. She looked off. "I heard from them," said Ettua. More money is not the answer. Was I misled by the cruelest path?

(Led)

I. Which statement is false? (a) A ribosome is smaller than a centriole. (b) Plant cells contain mitochondria. (c) A centriole contains microtubules. And II. How many people lived in the Caribbean region prior to the coming of the Europeans? III. Where are the furriest cats to be found in the wild? IV. What is the name of the mother of the man who first set foot on the moon? V. How many times can a flat pebble be skipped on the Dead Sea at noon in the third week of July if you have a flat pebble and the energy to skip it? Or VI. What is the smallest aperture leading to a discovery?

(Aperture)

Transfer not required between connecting routes. Heat makes your hair feel healthier. Transfers not transferable. "It's easy. It's so easy. Really, I can't believe how easy it is." Heat makes your hair feel healthier. Transfers not transferable. Don't listen to me. I do care, but don't listen to me. Don't listen to me. If it were not for the concluding hurly-burly one could rest content. But: My Lord, I will be ruled. Vincent left his window sill and went back through the bedrooms. Vincent had a kin condition (something like a skin condition but unmedicable). He had brushes and he had plants. He had Artemisia. He had pants with holes in the knees (especially designed, very expensive) and he had desires. The forces leading to desires do not vary. Don't listen to me, I haven't spoken with him in a long time. The tide has turned. Don't listen to me. I don't know anything, and even if I do, she looked off. He had desires and he had sticks and he had volumes and he had locks of hair and he had zippers and he had finger polish and he had a list of telephone calls to make, telephone calls, telephone ... calls. He went back. "When are you going back?" she said and he went back. He had plants, Artemisia, yellow, but don't listen to me. It's not easy to prove effectiveness. And contrary to what is generally thought, transfer is not required between connecting routes. Transfers are not transferable. He had dreams that would not dissipate. Don't listen to me. He had waking dreams, like pineapples, but I was always the one in the black top hat. Dreams beset him as he walked in the olivier gardens, the olivier gardens spreading, and stumbled on the rounded paving stones. Don't listen, sex is sunlight. He had dreams, he had microphones, he had kosher salt. Don't listen to me. "When are you going back," she said and he went back. He had dreams, he had microphones. The forces leading to desire do not vary. Don't listen. Dreams beset him as he walked in the olivier gardens. I do count, but don't listen to me.

(Transfer)

Meat substitutes have been discussed above. The Fat List contains some surprises. Meat substitutes are not open to discussion. "I heard from them," said Ettua. "They spoke, I listened." A kettle steamed upon the hob. "It's easy. It's so easy." She could picture the headline, "More money is not the answer." His face was flushed as he scanned the Fat List. She could picture the headline as she scanned the Fat List. A kettle steamed upon the hob as they scanned the Fat List together. If it were not for the concluding hurly-burly one could rest content. Meat substitutes are gaining in popularity. Meat substitutes are getting a good deal of attention. The tide has turned. She looked off. If it were not for the concluding hurly-burly one could rest content. He stared at her. Meat substitutes not the answer, Artemisia not the answer, mitochondria, contrary to popular surmise, not the answer, music not the answer, not even hurly-burly, not even Vincent, who went back, truth serum not the answer, perhaps more money—is that the answer? If it were not for the concluding hurly-burly one could rest content. I was always the man in a black top hat. He's just not picking up the ball. If it were not for the concluding hurly-burly one could rest content. "I can't say," she said. He's just not using the Fat List. Don't listen. If it were not for the concluding hurly-burly one could rest content. If it were not for the concluding hurly-burly one could rest. He's batting .394 but he's just not picking up the ball, and he's not on the Fat List, and he's not using meat substitutes, and he's not leaving. Don't listen, I wouldn't listen. If it were not for the concluding hurly-burly one could rest content. The Fat List notwithstanding, much needs to be done, and if you go it would be better for you to leave early, and there is a train at one. If you go it would be better. There is a train, the Fat List notwithstanding.

(The Fat List)

He had taken the virginity of the woman destined to become the wife of Henry of France. Whoosh, there it is. He fed her carrots so she would see when he blew out the candle. He pulled a fine silk thread around his balls, swelling them with desire. The musician playing the viol chuckled. His face was flushed. He bade her stroke his calves. She stared off. I could see a tiny blood vessel throbbing in his temple. She ran a hand over soft red leather. He had won through a chair back. Don't listen. She stared off. "My Lord, I will be ruled," she gasped, "My Lord, I will be ruled. My Lord, I will be ruled," she gasped, "My Lord I will be ruled." "How will you go, or will you go at all?" Ximena Flaviana Marquesa inquired playfully. They led him to the gallows, then led him away. "My Lord, I will be ruled," she gasped, "My Lord, I will be ruled. My Lord, I will be ruled," she gasped, "My Lord, I will be ruled. I will be ruled. I will. I will be on the train. My Lord, I will be ruled on the train. My Lord! I will!" They led him to the gallows, then led him away. They tied a thread around his balls, swelling them with method. Ever since then the tide has turned. More money is not the answer. "My Lord, I will be ruled!" The musician playing the viol chuckled. He was tied at the knees and elbows. A broth was prepared. If it were not for the concluding hurly-burly it would have been possible to rest content. There was a curious wooden bench and they sat him there, his balls dropping into a hole that had been bored. The princess spoke very clearly: "It's easy. It's so easy. I can't believe how easy it is." I was always the man in a black top hat. I could see a tiny blood vessel throbbing in his temple. I thought he was rather a handsome fellow. A kettle steamed upon the hob.

(Hurly-burly)

He's just not picking up the ball. She felt the soft leather and gave instructions and he took instructions and they delivered Artemisia but he's just not listening and with the concluding hurly-burly it's hard to discover whether or not they called. "They called," said Ettua. He's just not picking up the ball. He's batting .394 and he came over in trade for Okota but there's no way around it, he's just not picking up the ball. Radwanski is 4 for 11 with 111 career losses. "They definitely called," said Ettua, definitively. Vincent went back.

(.394)

They will be led, swiftly, by the cruelest path. Which statement is false? Which statement is false? Which statement is false or not false? Which statement is either not false or else false? Transfer not required between connecting routes. He had taken the virginity of the woman destined to become the wife of Henry of France. The musician playing the viol chuckled. "I heard from them," said Ettua. "From *them*." Heat makes your hair feel healthier. His face was flushed, and I could see a tiny blood vessel throbbing in his temple. A ribosome is smaller than a centriole. "It's easy. It's so easy." She ran a hand over the soft red leather. "How will you go, or will you go at all?" Ximena Flaviana Marquesa inquired deftly. He's just not picking up the ball. A centriole contains microtubules. One could rest content if it were not for the obstructions. "It's easy. It's so easy." His face was thoroughly flushed and I could see more than I wanted to see, more than he wanted me to see, more than she wanted him to want me to see, more than she wanted me to see, more than I would have wanted her to see, more than I wanted to see, more than she wanted to see. He had taken her virginity. The tide turned. For his part, he was as otherworldly as ever. "It's easy. It's so easy. I can't believe how easy it is," said the bastards in the green vests.

(Green Vests)

They said the northern cod stock was growing when it was actually sliding. It was very difficult either to assess or to reconnoiter. She could picture the headline, "More money is not the answer." His face was flushed. More money will not help. She looked off. Nothing will help but more money, yet more money will not help, and so nothing will help, but more money will actually not help. The northern cod stock is either growing or sliding. They said it was growing when it was sliding; but they have said it was sliding when it was growing. It is either growing or it is sliding at each moment. The northern cod stock might help but it is sliding, yet they said it was not sliding. I heard them. They were most definitive. "The northern cod stock is not sliding." Northern cod grows and slides. Nothing will help but more money and more money will not help. The northern cod stock is not growing but they said it was growing, but it is also not sliding and they did not say it was not sliding. The northern cod stock will not help. The northern cod stock is growing and sliding incalculably. They did not say it was not growing or not sliding and they did not say it was growing but not sliding or sliding but not growing or even not growing but also not sliding. "They called," said Ettua. They did not say it was growing. Meat substitutes, the cod stock, the Fat List, money—not the answer. She said she was sliding but actually she was growing but they said she was sliding but she will not help. He stared at her. Supposedly we can speed up the estimations. If it were not for the concluding hurly-burly, one could rest content. Supposedly the northern cod stock can accurately be estimated. Northern cod stock a problem. Northern cod stock a challenge. "Easy, so easy. I can't believe how easy." We are averaging over three hours a game, with or without the northern cod stock. We are averaging three hours and fourteen minutes a game, with or without the conversations and the conversions and whether the northern cod stock is growing or sliding. I was always the man in the black top hat. I'd cut it down if it were up to me, but there you are, we're averaging three hours and plus a game, and somebody doesn't want to do anything about it. The conversations are intolerable, and we are averaging three hours and plus and there you are. The hurly-burly is a problem. She held the hand strap. Nothing will help but more money, but they said, both officially and unofficially, "Money is not the problem." They said the northern cod stock was growing when it was actually sliding. Microtubules.

(The Northern Cod Stock)

I could see a tiny blood vessel throbbing in his temple. Transfers not transferable. Transfer not required between connecting routes. The Fat List contains some surprises. I thought he was rather a handsome fellow. Vincent left his window sill and went back through the bedrooms to the kitchen. "I heard from them," said Ettua. She will update us and we will update you and you can update them and they will update the audience. A tiny blood vessel appears to be throbbing. Transfer between connecting routes is advised. "I did hear from them," Ettua said, "I did." The Fat List contains as surprises petroleum products applied to the skin, including shaving creams. And tomatoes. Transfer is, in general, not required. "I heard from them," said Ettua. "I heard from them." Transfer neither required nor transferable. A tiny blood vessel was throbbing, I saw it, and his perspiration was flowing and he clenched his fists. Vincent left the window sill once and for all. A tiny blood vessel was throbbing, I saw, he clenched his fists, he seemed to be a rather handsome fellow, and he said, "The

Fat List contains some surprises, including crackers, including all crackers." All crackers, emphatic. But I could see a tiny blood vessel throbbing in his temple. I could see a tiny blood vessel. See, not detect; it didn't need detecting. He stared. I could see him stare. He stared, he clenched his fists. Once and for all he returned to the bedroom. All crackers, all crackers were on the Fat List. He stared. He had Artemisia. A tiny blood vessel was throbbing. He stared at her. Don't listen to me, there's no point listening to me. Don't. I've told you. I do care but I don't know. Even if I knew I wouldn't say. I would care but I wouldn't say. So don't listen. A tiny blood vessel was throbbing. Don't listen. Don't listen.

(Throbbing)

I could see a blood vessel throbbing in his temple, which proved that although he thought he was growing, nevertheless he was sliding. It is difficult to estimate whether one is sliding when one thinks one is growing, plain and simple, or growing when—and even as—one thinks one is growing. And even more difficult is ascertaining, actually ascertaining, the situation, this being partly due to the general condition which causes all of us to slide when we are certain that we grow, and also to slide when we are certain that we slide. We grow, but we also slide. In deference to the experts, who are often telephoning on Sundays, we slide more than we grow, and our tendency to grow is often masked by our tendency to slide. This is not to say that we do not grow. Indeed, we do grow, and grow surreptitiously, too, but even this growth is a kind of sliding, and in truth we slide even as we consider that we grow. Perhaps it is true that we never slide more than when we consider that we grow. Considering that we grow is not growing. Think of turnips. There was a small blood vessel throbbing in his temple, and I saw it. The soup boiled. He said, "I feel myself slipping," which is not the same as sliding, and the experts, who had called on Sunday, said, "Put ice." Perhaps they thought he meant he felt himself sliding, but sliding isn't slipping. Sliding isn't slipping, slipping isn't sliding. Note pads tumbled into the garbage, I'll tell you. The experts called only on Sundays, and often offered expertise where no expertise was demanded, and offered opinions about growing and sliding and about blood vessels swelling in one's temples. All of this information was placed on disk by people who drank from striped mugs. Sanctum sanctorum.

(Slipping and Sliding)

It's not easy to prove the effectiveness of a custom creation. We bought shirts. One shirt was peacock blue. She ran a hand over the soft leather of her pocketbook, the red leather, thinking of the odd trinkets she had dropped into it. She could picture the headline. A kettle steamed upon the hob. Heat makes your hair feel healthier. I was always the man in a black top hat. "I heard from them," said Ettua. "I heard," Ettua said. For his part, he was as otherworldly as ever, switching styles from transmuted alien peregrinations to his trademark drone throbs. It's not just the velocity that gives a hitter a problem. He's batting .394 but it's not just the velocity. It's the velocity but it's not just the velocity. He's batting .394 now, who knows about later? Who knows? Who knows about later, who knows about now? Who knows about the northern cod stock? Who knows about the Artemisia? Who knows about the kettle? A kettle steamed, who bought the kettle? We know who brought the kettle, but who bought the kettle? We walked past the Artemisia and went in. She looked off.

(Velocity and Kettle)

Examination:

[I] Which statement is false? (a) A ribosome is smaller than a centriole. (b) He had taken the virginity of a woman who was destined. (c) The musician playing the viol chuckled. (d) Plant cells contain mitochondria. (e) She ran a hand over her red leather pocketbook. (f) Transfer not required between connecting routes. (g) More money is not the answer. (h) She could picture the headline. (i) A kettle steamed upon the hob. (j) A centriole contains microtubules. (k) Heat makes your hair feel healthier. (l) They will be led, swiftly, by the cruelest path. (m) Dogs prefer cats to people.

[II] Which statement is true? (a) He took the virginity of a woman destined to become the wife of Henry of France. (b) A centriole is smaller than any dog. (c) Heat is unhealthy in the summer and healthy in the winter. (d) Mitochondria is a Japanese dog food. (e) The viol is a contemporary instrument of beautification. (f) For his part, he was as otherworldly as ever, switching styles from transmuted alien dances to his trademark olive paste. (g) I was always the man in a black top hat. (h) I was always the man in the pebble blue turtleneck. (i) Meat substitutes are dangerous. (j) He was rather a handsome fellow. (k) They did not have a kettle.

[III] They said the northern cod stock was growing when in actuality it was sliding. Discuss this statement, with reference to (i) fat, (ii) truth, (iii) virginity, (iv) centrioles, (v) cruelty, (vi) headlines, (vii) otherworldliness, (viii) black top hats.

[IV] "I was always the man in a black top hat." What are the implications of this statement?

[V] Was I misled?

(Examination)

Dream in Honor of Walter Benjamin

There is a secret, wrote Poe, that will not permit itself to be told, but surely I have been trying to tell it. In the end I suppose the best of capability will turn only to circumlocution, for the thing will hide itself when I approach. But it is not me, that I am clumsy or that I walk with too conspicuous a tread. The elusiveness is in the thing itself, the object of my flirtations. It has to do with flowers, precisely with the color of flowers, that cannot be spoken. And it inheres as well in the rhythmic fluctuations of the patterns of light upon surfaces, the reflections of ferns against a yellow wall, or the shimmers on the surface of the sea. There was a room in the basement of a building, with a cold, damp cement floor and no light. A high window let in the afternoon sun which cut in sharp angles across a set of interlinking chambers made of slatted wood, and padlocked, and filled with shadows and lampshades, boxes, dark jars filled to bursting with preserves. It was impossible for me to crack open the locks, to enter the chambers, to hunt through the layers of merchandise for the sacred envelope, the telling object; I could not return it to the light of day and tell its proper story; and so all that remains is the map of the chamber, the layout of the little rooms, the faded paint on the slats, the overpowering smell of mildew, and the occasional web of a spider. I am certainly a spy, but who is employing me? This is the question that has plagued my adult life. I have traveled an itinerary, catching exact views, and I have a catalogue, but I do not recognize the secret that I have encoded, and I do not know who is planning to extract it from me in the final analysis, or to what advantage they will do so. The facts I have collected have no shape that I can discern, yet their vitality impels me to protect them: if you have blond hair around your eyes, you will make a bad close-up; raisins should be added late to a batter; I should not fill up on cashews before dinner; my father had already done a day's work by nine o'clock in the morning; it was necessary for the director-general to meet with the entire staff; watermelon pickles were difficult to make well; one could lance a haematoma; after a hurricane, the beach sand would be glassine; the waters of the Baie des Anges are green; the waters off Nordwijk-an-see are slate blue, and the beaches are white, and Isadora Duncan danced there against the wind; a good Armagnac can be obtained near Hennequeville. Melody has always propelled me. Motive is an insoluble riddle, and we are never close to discerning why a man does what he does. I look up the skirt of a girl named Denyse and see her underwear, a kind of cul-de-sac, and all my wondering ends in wondering. A girl named Aloysha brings me to bed in a dark room, a hard bed, and she smells disturbingly of vanilla. Someone is always playing the piano in another room, blues, Debussy, Chopin's "Revolutionary" etude, Mozart's Sonata in F. A thief comes in through my window that leads out to a rooftop, stealing my ring. I walk into Riverside Park and am saddened by the long empty space, the assuredness of the river, the chestnut leaves, that a man is walking a little white dog. I take the greatest pleasure in savoring melancholy. I drift from setting to setting, searching for a key, and indeed I find it, and I have the key in my pocket; but what door does it open? I cannot make the necessary map because everything is out of order. The tall chimneys of the Con Ed facility near 14th St. cannot be placed in their proper position vis-à-vis my red pencils, my hammered copper pot from Dean and Deluca (big enough to float quenelles for half a dozen), the Long Man of

Wilmington, Walt Disney's *Peter Pan*. We tried to film a scene on a rooftop overlooking the Hudson, late in November and on an evening that had turned early to darkness. Rajiv came with his four vicious Dobermans (obedient as monks, when he spoke) and Neala made him tea with condensed milk and a bowl of rice. The dogs fell into a pile in a corner of the kitchen. Rajiv had lived here and then Ronald and Neala had taken the place over and Rajiv had moved to a gutted building on West 99th Street, where the dogs could ramble among the cold bricks and torn trapezia of wall board, and to which you gained entrance by dancing up a long sagging plank across a moat of broken stones and coiled wires covered with snow. The doves that Rajiv had kept (and sung to every evening) were Neala's now and she did not sing to them but she let Rajiv put some pieces of thawed frozen corn in their cage. We needed someone to hold a few branches over the heads of the boy and the girl as they turned against the darkness, and it began to snow heavily. Although Neala stood on a chair she could not get the branches to look properly in the viewfinder, so it took hours, and everybody was finally shivering, the boy and the girl particularly, as they had on the fawn costumes covered only by

blankets. Neala ran in and made hot chocolate.
Ronald said he didn't think there was enough film
for the number of takes we'd need. We got the shot,
but not until ten o'clock, and then everyone fell together into the room with the pink fabric draped
from the ceiling, the room where Ronald's library
sat in piles. Ronald put on Tony Bennett, very
loud. Rajiv and the dogs stood in the doorway, the
man fingering his proper Belgrade beard and looking puzzled. Neala brought out some dope and
rolled cigarettes which everybody smoked grate-
fully but me, and when I walked out, borrowing
Ronald's jacket, they were all in a half trance except
the dogs who were still wary and baring their teeth.
The park was an enchantment—Ronald lived near
106th St.—and I felt my body inside my clothes
warm and satisfied and the cold wind biting my
face. There was no hint of what would come next.
My telephone was ringing. It was Ronald's voice.
"Why did you leave?" I held the receiver in the
darkness, trying to think what to say. "I was tired."
He waited a moment and cleared this throat.
"That's really true?" I didn't have words. Outside
my window, across the chasm of darkness, a man in
a tank top was scrubbing his underarms with a
towel in a rectangle of orange light. "Rajiv thought

there was something wrong," Ronald's voice said. "He's gone with the dogs, if you want to come back." I hung up and lay for a long time on the bed in the darkness, smelling onions frying from across the veil of darkness. A siren wailed. I walked back to Ronald's, against the fierce wall of snow that was blowing down. The boy and the girl were asleep next to the dove cage in the kitchen, wrapped into one another under a gray blanket. Neala and Ronald were moaning in the bedroom. I sat listening to Miles Davis, reading Petrarch and then Joseph Conrad and then J. D. Salinger. Ronald came out wearing a towel around his waist. "We are going to have to do something with you and your indiscriminate life," he said. I got on a bus the next day and rode into the mountains, west, northwest, anywhere to get away from Ronald, yet I could hardly say as much to myself. Pennsylvania was nothing but a nondescript obstruction that seemed to hold us back, and the bus crept higher and higher into the Poconos and wound its way west. I forget where we stopped after that. I sat in a coffee shop twirling my spoon in an empty mug. In Los Angeles there was a show of African masks in a museum next to the tar pits. I headed south to Mexico and rode many buses of many colors into many provinces with many kinds of cactus, and recognized none of the emotions brushed onto the broad faces of the other riders. I wrote a letter to Ronald and Neala, thanking them for everything and wishing them success, and I put this in a mailbox. I wondered whether he'd ever get the film cut, and whether he'd find someone to release it. The boy and the girl were plenty good. I remember being invited home for dinner by a taco seller near a fountain in the center of a village that has no name. He gave me something strong to drink. I awoke and he was lying next to me on a bed. I asked him what he was doing and he said, "What do you mean?" I remember running. He called after me. I must have taken a bus, there is no memory, but the chapter, like a long precarious note on a saxophone, ended and I was in New York again, in the spring. I phoned Ronald and there was no answer, day or night, and at his apartment there was no response when I rang and then climbed up and pounded on the door. Years later, I learned that Ronald and Neala had split, had split that very night, that she had gone to Massachusetts and he had followed me to Los Angeles and had disappeared soon after arriving. The compass for me had contracted to a point. I spent the days sitting on a bench in the middle of

Broadway, near the 72nd St. subway. The other men sitting around me, with their *Times*, were old and unshaven, wearing ancient torn tweed overcoats and half-melted sneakers, muttering in Russian and Yiddish, men who smelled of sour cream and radishes and frowned at me and slept through the afternoons. Then, as though in some kind of finale, a taxi pulled up. A girl got out with a cello case. She started talking to me, talking about nothing, then we hailed a cab and rode to her apartment on 104th near Riverside. A classy building. She was very strange, never wanting to stop talking to me, never wanting to look at me. "Elaine," she said when I asked her name. I took a pencil and conducted her while she practiced Prokofiev's sonata. "Your downbeat," said she, "is weak." We lay together on her sofa. "We can get married if you like," came out of her mouth. I waited until it registered and that is what it sounded like. I went downtown to retrieve my things from a locker in the Port Authority and when I came back, maybe an hour later, her door was bolted. I knocked as loudly as I could without making a scene. I put my mouth near the lip of the door and said, "What are you doing? Let me in. Elaine—" She opened the door but kept it on the chain. Her face was painted with mascara and very dark lipstick, unintelligible, and there was malevolence in her eyes. "Listen," she said with a kind of hoarse voice, "Listen: My name isn't Elaine. I made that up. Now, go away. I don't want to see you anymore. Don't make trouble. If you need money, I'll give you some. Somebody is here. You'd better not stay. I've . . ." and this sounded very much like a gun going off, "changed my mind." We had played for a week, which flew by now in a flash. Spring exploded. I got a job in a record store near Columbus Circle and at night I went to the Thalia and saw every film by Godard and Chris Marker and Claude Chabrol and Vittorio De Sica. I took a bus out to Glen Cove to see Ronald's parents, who said a letter had come for me. It wasn't from Ronald, it was from Neala, and there were only a few lines. "Life always seems to be a mystery when we don't know who we are," was the ending, I'll never forget that. She had underlined the "seems." I asked where Ronald was and they said, honestly I think, that they didn't know, but that Neala had left him, not the other way around, and that he had been turned upside-down. "He was with the wrong people," said his father. He poured us glasses of Bourgeuil and we drank them slowly, the old man waving a hand through his thick hair and asking me what I was going to do with my life. I went up to Ronald's room, which by now had been taken over by Eric, his brother. It was beyond spotless. The maroon bedspreads were pulled taut on the twin beds. The bookshelves were practically empty. There was a plastic model of the USS Constitution, that Ronald had built as a boy. I went through the desk drawers, but there was nothing of Ronald's, in fact nothing at all. In the closet there was no shirt pocket with a note, no folded map. I looked out the window at the carefully designed garden and the Lincoln Continental in the driveway. A groundskeeper was watering the hydrangea towers. There was nothing to do now but bring the curtain down. I retreated, took the L. I. R. R. back to the city, stayed on at the record shop for another couple of weeks, hearing those who spoke to me as if they were under water, then packed a bag, took the train up to the George Washington Bridge, and went by foot across the steaming river. I didn't turn back, yet I could see nothing before me but the indiscriminate gliding of trucks and the silent soaring of gulls. He will be at the toll booths, I assured myself, imagining that I was approaching Checkpoint Charlie and he was my runner waiting to bring me across and home. But of course he wasn't. At the toll plaza it was impossible to get a ride, so I hiked down the road a bit and finally got picked up not far east of Englewood. Everywhere flat warehouses, neon signs for gas stations off the road. What kind of vehicle it was, what sort of driver, what direction, I cannot—nor want to—recall. It was the first in a chain of trucks and beat-up cars that began all those years ago, chaining themselves across the states and states of mind, and that have finally delivered me here, here in front of your face, after the shapeless circumlocution which has been my query and my fate.

Dreams from Voskresenskoye

"WHY

take the stairs," she said, "when you can take the lift?" She was carrying the thinnest imaginable candle. "When the lift is there, why take the stairs?" Wilted lettuce was something she couldn't bring herself to touch. Under any circumstances. On one occasion, a whole lot of butterflies came in and floated around, but we managed to eat. She had to repeat herself because no one behaved as though he had been listening, and Krasnovskoy, in fact, was tippling over into a snore, his usual. Likewise Tiptin. "Why take the stairs when you can take the lift? It's a general question, not a particular one. It's a general *type* of question. It's a question I always ask in life, at every peculiar moment in its peculiar way. Is it that I have a penchant for the modern, do you think? Is that what it is? The lift was hugely costly, you know. And it's nothing if not the newest fashion, that's true enough. But it's a question I'm always asking in life: when you can take the lift, why take the stairs? One never has quite enough money to purchase furniture." She was right, it was a question she asked always, one way or another, as though filtering or resolving all of experience into a single precarious, delicious bubble. Krasnovskoy is no dilettante. Likewise Tiptin. Increasingly paranoid and reclusive, that one has spent the past three months recalibrating the tumblers on all the locks. Slowly he pushed himself up and stumbled over to the eastern wall. He took down a Bakst watercolor. He brought it to the table and leaned it against the carafe of anisette. "Why take the stairs when you can take the lift?" she said again, like a parrot, but this time he glared quite rashly at her, "For heaven's sake, Katerina Petrovna, you have had the trough dismantled. Now where will the horses drink?"

THE FINELY CHISELED

expression of exalted consciousness is not unlike the look of stupidity, he read, and then closed the book, a difficult enough task since the binding was gone, and looked out at the wind callously blowing through the trees, then blew his nose, and thought he caught a whiff of rosemary from somewhere beneath his feet. Stones from the quarry, decades ago, with rosemary and some thyme oozing up in the cracks between. Slowly he pushed himself up and stumbled over to the eastern wall. While the family happily ignored part of the garden when the peak of its season was done, the paying visitors wanted perfection everywhere. She would be quite capable of arranging everything tomorrow, were it not for the fact that people were waiting for her in Voskresenskoye and that she absolutely had to fly off without delay. Long coat, silk scarf, even her extended hands trailing behind in the breeze. Well, one never has quite enough money to purchase furniture. We all become children again when we go to sleep.

PAYING

visitors wanted perfection everywhere. We all become children again when we go to sleep. Somewhat shaken, you enter by way of a central French window done up in vermilion. Spontaneity certainly brings drawbacks. On one occasion a whole lot of butterflies came in and floated round, but we managed to eat. Tiptin rested. We put up a long piece of string between one position and the other. The quavery meow of a cat issued from a pyramid of damson-colored cushions. The lily symbolized fertility. Old Pulyakin says he is in no way offended when people say his apartment possesses a charm that borders on the feminine. "Those were the most vivid years of our lives." Slowly he pushed himself up and stumbled over to the eastern wall. She would be quite capable of arranging everything tomorrow, were it not for the fact that people were waiting for her in Voskresenskoye and that she absolutely had to fly off without delay. Spontaneity certainly brings drawbacks. The quavery meow of a cat issued from a pyramid of damson-colored cushions. On one occasion a whole lot of butterflies

came in and floated round, but we managed to eat.
Those were the most vivid years of our lives. Lippi
Yuriatnikoff painted his walls the same color as his
ceiling; or his ceiling the same color as his walls; in
the end they were the same, and they faded together, but he was gone to the summer palace and he
treasured the color they had been long before, the
green of parrots.

HERBS

and ferns, buddleia and mimosa, wisteria and clematis, hydrangea and pepperwort—everything was there. "Those were the most vivid years of our lives." Somewhat shaken, you enter by way of a central French window done up in vermilion, all vermilion, swagged in vermilion. She painted the priest's house oyster white. Spontaneity certainly brings drawbacks. Somebody will eventually get around to reparations. He will have nothing to do with the end of our century. "We were at the epicenter," explains Anna Madrigalya Roshov calmly. She is sublime. Katerina Petrovna Piripin isn't listening, hanging up handkerchiefs on a line she's strung between one position and another in the straw barn. The quavery meow of a cat came out. "We were at the epicenter of epicenters, and even that didn't make us happy," Anna Madrigalya is nibbling strudel, "And that is what is wrong with us." He took down a Bakst watercolor for her, nibbling strudel. Somewhat shaken, you enter by way of a central French window. The vermilion is staggering. We all become children again when we go to sleep. The furniture comes in pairs. Slowly he pushed himself up and stumbled over to the eastern wall. In the center of the eastern wall was a French window. We all become children again when we go to sleep. Snow may arrive any time after the first day of November. She would be quite capable of arranging everything tomorrow. You enter by way of a central French window. She is sublime. He is not a dilettante. She is not listening, nibbling strudel. He is holding back from smoking a cigar. After the first flush of delight came a cold shower of reappraisal. She had French roots on her mother's side and Russian ones on her father's, and she had a room full of Dalís and another room full of Fayard du Bourgos. Tiptin swung back and forth in his hammock, watching the movement of a mosquito on his upper arm.

ONE

teepee is all the staking necessary, you know, for a quartet of tomato plants. The furniture comes in pairs.

"WE

were at the epicenter," explains Anna Madrigalya calmly. The house was full of chickens. The lily symbolized fertility. Cattle surrounded us, but at a distance. The quavery meow of a cat issued from a pyramid of cushions. The staircase wound past a guest room once employed as a store for olives. Kuleshov laid down his ace. Natural dyes were mostly abandoned at the beginning of the twentieth century. Spontaneity certainly brings drawbacks. One never has quite enough money to purchase furniture. "I really didn't know I had so much capital," says Kuleshov. The finely chiseled expression of exalted consciousness is not unlike the look of stupidity, he read. She would be quite capable of arranging everything tomorrow, were it not for the fact that people were waiting for her. She painted the priest's house oyster white. Snow may arrive any time after the first day of November. If she were a vegetable, she'd certainly be a radish. "We were at the epicenter," explains Anna Madrigalya quite calmly, "But Voskresenskoye was at the margins." He took down a Bakst watercolor. One never has quite enough money to purchase furniture. One tepee really is all the staking necessary for a quartet of tomato plants. Somewhat shaken, you enter by way of a central French window, the holy vermilion. While the family happily ignored part of the garden when the peak of its season was done, the paying visitors wanted perfection everywhere. He will have nothing to do with the end of our century. The death knell for modernism was sounded, perhaps, by the sour cream sitting frankly upon the onions. He says he is in no way offended when people say his apartment possesses a charm that borders on the feminine. Somebody will eventually get around to reparations. Erich von Stroheim used real caviar and champagne in his party scenes, but his actors were not allowed to actually eat or drink.

SOMEWHAT

shaken, you enter by way of a central French window. All around us thatch is glistening because
of the heavy rains. On one occasion a whole lot
of butterflies came in and floated round, but we
managed to eat. She would be quite capable of arranging everything. The finely chiseled expression
of exalted consciousness is not unlike the look of
stupidity. Why take the stairs when you can take
the lift?

SNOW

transformed everything into an abstraction of lines and shadows. The quavery meow of a cat issued from a shadow bordered by lime trees now denuded. They really didn't know they had so much. Bakst watercolors were piled in the corners of all the rooms. None of them were dilettantes. Snow transformed even the handkerchiefs drying on the line strung between one position and another in the straw barn. The quavery meow of a cat issued again. Snow transformed the darkness, purified it, rendered the darkness as shadows and lines, illuminated the stars, made the stars dense with effect, condensed the stars, chilled the vacuum in which the condensed stars shone, rendered the stars as points, camouflaged the watercolors, and lines were strung from one position to another. "Voskresenskoye must be preserved at all costs," said Anna Madrigalya Roshov but Katerina Petrovna Piripin wasn't listening, she was searching for the cat. Old Muffik lit an extremely thin candle. The snow rendered the scurrying form of Katerina Petrovna Piripin as a shadow and a line as she hur-

ried to boil dumplings for the men coming in from
the hunt. Voskresenskoye faded into the darkness
rendered by snow, the opalescent darkness rendered by unanticipated snow.

THE FURNITURE

comes in pairs. "I really didn't know I had so much capital," says Vassily Lermonteyev Kuleshov, who is surely not a dilettante. Wilted cabbage. That was something he couldn't bring himself to touch. Not now, not ever. Wilted to any degree. At any of the numerous stages of wilting. Spontaneity certainly brings drawbacks. One never has quite enough money to purchase furniture. He took down a Bakst watercolor. Increasingly paranoid and reclusive, he has spent the past six months recalibrating the tumblers on all his locks. We spoke frequently of stopping the affair, but business got in the way, and there were complications. Dossiers were sealed. Tiptin rolled over. After the first flush of delight came a cold shower of reappraisal. Vassily Lermonteyev Kuleshov laid down his ace. "I really didn't know I had so much capital." Katerina Petrovna Piripin isn't listening. We look slowly around the room—it is an enormous room by any standards—and see that the furniture comes in pairs.

THE CHILDREN WERE ON THE BENCH

by the lake, we called them the children, they were imprisoned by the isosceles triangle of moonlight, we called them children but they had entered the world, you could have fried an egg on that bench, the moonlight was positively green, they had lips only for one another, they had lips. Tiptin watched them, they walked as if in a dream and fell onto the bench by the lake, it wasn't really a lake but it was a fattening of a river, we called it the lake, we called them children, they said it would be a good idea to go swimming—swimming now at midnight—but one was too heavy and the other too light, we call them children. The moon was positively green. The green moon of Voskresenskoye. An isosceles triangle on the lake surface, near the boats, and a balalaika off in the distance, and somebody starts quoting a very bad translation of Baudelaire which seems out of place. "Bonjour mademoiselle," it's possible to hear, "Bonjour, bonjour, ma jolie mademoiselle."

IF

Anna Madrigalya Roshov were a vegetable, she'd certainly be a radish. She painted the barber's house oyster white. Like the priest's. Snow may arrive any time after the first day of October. While the family happily ignored part of the garden when the peak of its season was done, paying visitors wanted perfection everywhere. A purity of snow fell and transformed us. Snow rendered the paying visitors as lines and shadows. All around us, thatch is glistening because of the heavy rains that washed away the snow. Conversation was mostly abandoned at the beginning of the twentieth century. She had French roots on her mother's side and Russian ones on her father's. Somebody will eventually get around to reparations. We all become children again when we go to sleep. She would be quite capable of arranging everything tomorrow but she must fly off. They are waiting for her at Voskresenskoye. Scarf in the wind. He took down a watercolor by Bakst, "Summer at the Lake." The death knell for modernism was sounded. Snow may arrive anytime. Somewhat shaken, you enter by way of a central French window.

Dream Lillebrød

Lillebrød (strictly, "little bread") are tiny Scandinavian tales, like hors d'oeuvres of the imagination.

TWO NEIGHBORING DAIRY FARMERS

pastured their cows on the same rich grass. When it was announced that the Queen was to be married, they decided to conjoin their milk and fabricate for her the greatest of all cheeses.

Day and night they worked, consuming much Port, and it is true the cheese they made was both gigantic and magnificent.

They covered it round with sheets of muslin and then sealed it in a pearwood box big enough to hold clothing for a trip to India.

A letter on vellum came from the High Chamberlain. "Her Majesty is struck silent and commands me to convey to you her thanks for an article the like of which has never been seen in the Court. The bearer delivers to you two new pennies."

The pennies shone in the afternoon sunlight, each happily embossed with a portrait of the Queen.

"At Her Majesty's Agricultural Fair," the farmers wrote back to the High Chamberlain, "we would propose to exhibit this cheese. May we have Royal Permission? This product is a testament to our pride, and to our great admiration and love for the Queen."

A letter of permit was delivered the same day by horsemen to each farmer, with a waxen seal, and on the morning of the third day afterward the testamentary cheese itself arrived from the palace, still in its pearwood box, upon a cart drawn by six horses with purple plumes. The equerry assisted in depositing this great object on the ground at the side of the road, near the tiny rivulet where two modest gates led away to the two farms.

"I am right pleased, Maggam," said one farmer to his friend.

"Pleased as punch, Derby," said the other.

A week quietly passed.

"I will be satisfied, Maggam," said Derby, as they sat upon a great stone thinking about the Fair, "to win a medal for this great exemplar of the cheesemaker's art."

Maggam sat chewing grass for a long, silent moment. "You what then?"

"I will be satisfied. I will be pleased. This great example. The cheesemaker's art."

"'Tis surely *I* who would have that pleasure, friend Derby," said Maggam. "'Tis *here*," he tapped his skull, "that resides the cheesemaker's art of which you speak. Forget ye not, my milk is the dominating milk in that 'ar cheese. Thar be no question at all of domination, since it be plain as grass."

"What's yer lips?" said Derby, rather too crisply, giving a quite penetrating squint. Evidently a storm was brewing. "*Mine* is the finer herd, man. *Mine* was the richer milk. Was, friend Maggam. Was, *dear* friend Maggam. *My* hands were always the harder working hands of the four, friend Maggam. Were mine."

"Der—by!" growled Maggam, turning his back.

"O thou Maggam!" winced Derby, turning his.

The many sons and daughters of Maggam and Derby came to augment their fathers' arguments, one team against the other, because a genetic honor was in question. The squabbling became loud and sharp. Sticks were taken to hand.

It was decided that nothing but a legal process could resolve the true authentic proprietorship of the greatness in the Queen's cheese, which thing, indeed, was still sealed in its box. On a flat wagon the great object was towed into the town and put for keeping at the Chief Magistrate's. Having begun, the process wound through many testimonies, many vituperations. Prolix prolixity of prolixness. The memoranda of record, penned in a flowing hand by the old clerk, Yprès, piled into seventeen bound volumes. Catalogued, wheeled away on trollies, shelved in semi-darkness. Years and years passed. Maggam put up a pointed fence to keep out Derby and Derby's issue, but Derby no longer went up to the hill where the greenest pasture lay, to smoke his pipe and stare blissfully at the sky. The children of Maggam and Derby married well enough, each to their own best advices, and produced grandchildren who learned to detest one another. And still the judiciary was not complete, because the lawyers on both sides—Crewell, Crewell, and Crewell acting for Maggam and Arbuthnot, Radingham, Radingham, and Smart acting for Derby—all retired themselves and were replaced by other lawyers—Seward, Seward, Seward, and Jaines on the one side; Proulme, Jebbons, and Lutyens on the other—who all died and were then replaced by Tewkesbury, Halywell, and Tewkesbury and Holywell, Talkston, and Holywell.

Soon, the Queen, married a long time and the producer of a colossal royal incorporation, four boys, four girls, who grew and married and augmented the thing, had quite forgotten about the great cheese.

Maggam took ill and died.

Derby sold his farm and moved with all his is-sue into the north country, Scarborough way.

The case of Maggam v. Derby was abandoned.

The cheese was never found in the repositories of the Chief Magistrate.

[Lillebrød of Maggam and Derby]

AT THE HÔPITAL DE LA SALPÊTRIÈRE IN PARIS,

a medical student named Longchamps sat diligently from morning until night listening to lectures and taking copious notes. Always he carried his chin rather high in the air, from pride at the august career that was impending. And from staying up reading by lamplight all night long his eyes were red and teary. At this great hospital, there was nothing they didn't teach him. This was the Salpêtrière, after all; there was nothing they didn't have, to teach.

But this is how the august medical career ended:

One day Longchamps was sitting in endocrinology class and the lecturer, a gaunt fellow with a goatee, Estimable Honorable Professor Doctor Parzul, was saying, "A woman will come into your examining room and you will see that her complexion is rather green, that her tongue is dry, that there is yellowing in her cornea, that her fingers twitch spasmodically, and that—"

"Mon Dieu!" said Longchamps to himself, lifting his pen abruptly from his notebook and turning to gaze out the window, where brown leaves were being blown from the branches of a great oak in a line of great oaks on the rue Jenner. "Mon Dieu, it is true! They will all be *sick!*"

Never before this moment had it occurred to him that once he was a doctor, the people he would see—all the people he would see—would be suffering. As to suffering, he had filed away ten thousand medical illustrations memorized from textbooks. With colorings orange and red and yellow and blue and black. And he had imagined that in his waiting room only beautiful ladies would sit, holding parasols, yellow with begonias printed, green with raindrops. But he saw now that his professional life was destined to be one lingering chain of sickness, sickness, sickness, and yet more sickness. He stood up, leaving the textbook behind him, and walked out of the lecture theater without looking back.

[Lillebrød of Endocrinology]

LABELLE,

a young lecturer in psychopathology at the Sorbonne, not yet with ribbons, had married and taken a very nice apartment in the rue Barbette. He spent long hours preparing his lectures, and began to develop, more and more, exactly the sort of enthusiasm for psychological derangement that is apposite in a brilliant lecturer with an office on the rue de l'École de Médecin but that his happy young wife could hardly bear. Marceline. What she loved was flowers, arrangements of flowers, paintings of arrangements of flowers, books about the history of flower arranging. And so she went to museums and libraries and often came home when already Labelle was sleeping.

He made a lot of money (oddly for a lecturer; but people wanted him badly to address audiences around the country, and were willing to pay).

One day, walking down the gray corridor to his office, he stumbled into a man with a long cigar. "Listen, *tiens*," said this one, "I'm looking for somebody who teaches psychology. Anybody like that around here? I'm a movie producer. I have come all the way from Hollywood. Don't have a lot of time to spare. Time is money."

The cigar, thought Labelle, was quite fetid, but he had to admit he loved movies and, as could be said of so many of his countrymen, his dreams took place in Hollywood. (Hollywood is, in fact, a dream being entertained in Paris.) So he said, "Me."

They got to talking and it turned out this man was producing a film in which no less than Brigitte Bardot was going to star as a professor of psychology who would be fascinated by various forms of psychological derangement and who would have an office on the rue de l'École de Médecin, so she needed somebody to talk to, upon whom she could in some ways model her performance. Brigitte Bardot herself, but oh yes. With her four cats. Soon, Labelle was nonplussed to see, she was sitting at the Café de la Paix, talking to him—she and no one else but she; him and no one else but him. He thought, "Delightful. She is a queen. A bouquet of sweet peas, such as my Marceline brings and puts in a little ceramic cup on the table. Intoxicating." So he shared with her, with the eager, the thirsty Brigitte, everything he knew, and she drank it up and bought him chocolates and a tisane of bergamot and took plenty of notes in a little book covered with red tissu de Souleiado. "D'accord. Oui. D'accord. Oui. Oui. Mais bien sûr. Oui oui. D'accord."

"I myself am tutoring Brigitte Bardot!" he planned to tell his wife, but she wasn't home and so he made himself an omelette fines herbes. Later, when Marceline came in, she was much too tired to hear about anything Labelle might relate because all day she had been reading about Alcibiades, a man who was obsessed with roses. Already in his bath, Labelle was dreaming of riding down the Champs Elysées in a limousine, with Bardot at his side, waving to a crowd.

To his class at the Sorbonne he made an announcement. "You will all undoubtedly think I am fabricating, but I have been engaged as special tutor to none other than Brigitte Bardot. And to me as a teacher she is very attracted. It will do you good to know that when I talk to her, she has no hesitation at all in taking notes, not like some people I have met." He gave them a frown. "We have formed a perfect relationship, Brigitte and I, and it is characterized by just a little fondness, you know, which is the spice of education. I may say, it is very likely that she will be waiting for me in my office when I return after this lecture, and that is why I must cancel my office hour today. In effect, she may also be waiting for me at a restaurant tonight. C'est comme ça. So, do not convince yourselves there is no practical use for a theory of psychopathology, because even now, through my personal influence, Brigitte Bardot is making use of one for a film you will all run out and pay to see. And by the way, we are on a first-name basis, she and I. Even better. I call her Petit Chat."

The three or four out of the group who were note-takers of course wrote all this down, although being but twenty or so, they really didn't have a clue who Brigitte Bardot was.

But at any rate, a strange and in some ways unfortunate thing happened. Brigitte Bardot, Petit Chat, began to enter all of Labelle's many conversations. He would say to his wife at breakfast, "Brigitte thinks we should find a little studio to work in, un petit atelier, maybe in the 7ème near the Champ de Mars." Or he would say, "Petit Chat likes confiture de poires."

Picking up some radishes for a salade composée, he would say to the greengrocer, old Monsieur Lafontaine, "Brigitte Bardot likes radishes, too."

And when speaking to his students of Freud

and Charcot he would intone, "Brigitte found Freud intriguing, but Charcot more intriguing, and both of them more intriguing that the other theorists I taught her."

The Chair of the Department would ask him to attend meetings of committees and he would answer, "Yes, yes, in principle; but I must wait to find out if Bardot requires me on that date."

In the echoing confines of his mind, as well, the man began to speak not only about Brigitte but also to her. And it is true that in that great chamber he would also hear her talking if not to then about him. She would say, "As he strolls down one side of the Place de la Madeleine, that intriguing Labelle is wondering whether he should perhaps dip into Fauchon and buy me a little bonbon in a pink box." She would also say, at the strangest and most unexpected moments, such as when he bent over to tie his shoe, "Fascinating thought! That Labelle, he is a fountainhead of fascinations." If, during a lecture, he made an exposition his students couldn't quite understand, Brigitte would happily sing out, "Oh yes! Beautifully beautifully beautifully expressed!"

She spoke to him in the middle of the night. "I'm so lonely!"

And while he was devouring a gratinée on the

Boul. Saint-Michel she would murmur, "Let's duck together into the Cluny and admire the tapestries!"

The poor fellow wiped his lips and went ducking into the Cluny, and climbed the dank steps into the great upper hall where the unicorn tapestries shone all ruby red in a humid little sepulcher of silence. "Look here, at the turn of the maiden's lip," Brigitte whispered to him. "See the agony in the posture of the hounds!"

Now she touched his hand and said she loved him, that she had tried to fight loving him but had been overwhelmed by his nobility, his intriguing smile, the fact that he smelled of pine. She drew herself very close to him, wrapping her body into the curl of his arm. She hung close to him as he walked back to the Sorbonne and entered the lecture theater, and stood in a shivering embrace with him at the front of the room as he addressed the students about forms of psychopathological delinquency. "O Brigitte, Brigitte!" cried he, as the students gaped, and he clutched her and drew his lips down to hers. "How I have fought this! I have fought this!" The note takers were getting writer's cramp, there was so much to quickly get down. "O Brigitte!"

When Brigitte struggled to pull her clothes off,

and to free him from his, the students made for
the doors. "Petit chat, petit chat," he told her, "Yes
yes. It is only appropriate and respectful that they
should accord us some privacy for the flowering of
our love."

It poured rain outside, and the note takers'
notebooks were drenched, the sentences drowned.
They looked at one another, trembling, as they
headed for the street.

[Lillebrød of the Agony of the Hounds]

A LONG TIME AGO, MEN

built a theater in Sablufft, our little village. The building is at the end of the main street, with an ornate stained glass transom over its main door and decorative brickwork gables under its lofty roof. One day a poster went up to say that Oliver Meisen—that's Sir Oliver Meisen—would appear to read Shakespeare and Goethe, Racine and Schiller, and Uls van Neumeyer. On the day of the performance, hundreds and hundreds of people were lined up in the street.

Far more were lined up than live in our village, in fact. The cars came from the south through the morning in an unbroken line, and were parked on the other side of the creek in the fields now cleared of corn. Oliver Meisen never gives performances. Never ever anywhere anytime.

Our village women put up booths and sold pasties and home-made wine.

By eventide, there were great roaring noises from the crowd outside the theater, and two jugglers started a bonfire and sang rowdy songs and a boy with his face painted white walked back and forth along the line doing pantomime and holding out his hat. This was Stälwart's boy, the mute, whose garish features were made beautiful in this masque. Night fell and the crowd was admitted to the theater.

A great tranquility fell upon the village at this point. Torches on poles dropped clouds of orange light upon the parked cars. One or two men hung about in the street, smoking. Most of the villagers, who could not afford to hear Oliver Meisen, sat at home listening to their radios.

But soon it became clear that something was untoward in the theater. Ten minutes or so after the performance was to have begun, the doors opened and two ushers came into the street, looking around with lines of anxiety etched on their cheeks. They went back inside, but soon came out again, this time with a manager in a tuxedo, Wallstein, who kept checking his watch. Oliver Meisen, it soon became evident, had not appeared. Through the open doors you could hear the rumbling of the great audience inside.

Rumbling—but no one left.

All these people—the hoi polloi who had brought lobster to eat from their Rolls Royces and the vacationers from Bad Saarsbeck and the office workers from Schmeningen—waited, then began to clap, and clap again, until there was a rhythm, a mantra, that became threatening. They grumbled. Then they shouted, "Hey Meisen, we not good enough for you?" to the man who wasn't there. Reporters from the local newspaper rushed in and wrote quickly in their notebooks. Telephone calls were made. Wallstein set foot on the huge stage, which was shiny and new, held up his plump little hands, and said, "Soon, soon he will come. He will come soon." He had a very musical voice altogether. "He will come. He will come." Late into the night, the audience continued to wait for the great Oliver Meisen, murmuring, shuffling, starting—some of them—to snore. (If he came he would sing, and if he sang they did not want to lose their precious seats.)

When by midnight he had not arrived, nor had there been received a single sign of him, they straggled away to their cars and drove away from our village. The theater lights were turned out and the doors were locked. The torches in the cornfield were extinguished.

In the morning, men arrived from the great newspapers in the city, asking, Why had Oliver Meisen not arrived? They asked Wallstein and our

Mayor, Skägen, and the Director of our Chamber of Commerce, Poojt, and Remnans, the Chief of Police, but of course not one of these had the ghost of an idea. They then went around interviewing everyone they could find, "Why did he not arrive?" and as no one had an interesting thought the reporters made up thoughts of their own and soon enough—it didn't take a week—our little village was at the center of a great national mystery. The greatest actor of the age had vanished into thin air, right here, in Sablufft. The theater was dismantled, board by board, because it now came out—and this was most odd, that it was said only *after* all the commotion—that Sir Oliver Meisen had been waiting alone in his dressing room. He had been in the building. He had been there. But then, just as time came for him to step onto the stage, he had disappeared. Pooft! How on earth could a man vanish! And so august a man as Sir Oliver! They lifted the boards, every board, and unlocked all the doors in the basement, and looked in the attic, and looked, too, in every house in the village, and also in the surrounding fields, and in the woods of Deldomminen, and on the other side of the great river Tipo in the three great clearings, but there wasn't an Oliver Meisen to be found.

The poster is still there, in many vitrines. Oliver Meisen will read Shakespeare, Goethe, Racine, Schiller, and Van Neumeyer. And sing. Read and sing. Sing and read. Books have been written about the vanishing of Oliver Meisen. Next to the spot where the theater doors once stood, in a wooden cabinet beautifully designed, there is a plaque. All around town, fixed behind glass, the poster yellows.

[Oliver Meisen Lillebrød]

A MAN AND WOMAN STOOD BESIDE

Lake Tuorminen, staring a little past one another at the mist screening the placid water. Yawning off into the vapors were blue pines. A loon cried twice.

He wondered whether he should touch her arm, which was bent a little at the elbow in the oversized tweed coat that had been her husband's. He wondered whether any good could come of him saying now, "I thought I knew him." There were no tears on her face. Her cheeks were smooth the way wood much polished by being rubbed in the hand is, and again the loon cried twice. He wondered whether he should say, "I took his ring because I thought he would have wanted me to have it, and I thought he knew he was dying and would be calmed to know his ring had been taken." She looked quickly at him, her eyes dark chestnuts without fire. He kept silent.

"You have become him," she said finally, clasping her white long fingers together. "Through the years I saw the resemblance shaping and contorting, and as he faded I saw you ascending, and now you have become all that he was. His students

will be your students. You will write the books he
would have written."

He wondered if he should tell her he had taken
the ring.

[Lillebrød of the Lake]

THE TWO GROINS

of the lovers were locked helplessly, and the coils of groin hair pulled off in the struggle for independence scattered upon the sheets. The working of the hips together was blunt, hopeless, unintelligent, quick, arrogant. Each of them wore over the ears a slender set of headphones and a microphone, wired to a telephone. Each leaned back, supporting a posture with fingertips. Every nuance of breath was broadcast to the hidden audience of two. In a bowl on a nearby table two goldfish hunted through fronds of Artendoria pladentes, shuddering at the tail. One lover saw from the corner of a moss green eye a yellow notepad and a pencil that would soon be used for making a shopping list. "Si fuentes espladoria," sighed the other. There is a passage somewhere in Shostakovich with a solo flute, and from somewhere outside it could now be heard.

[Lillebrød of the Duet]

"THERE IS A WONDERFUL

motion picture by Jean Renoir," said Barouche to Leung. "I forget the name of it. It plays down the street at the Odéon. Quite a marvel. In fact, delirious. You should go to see it."

Because Barouche was a fop whose taste was not to be emulated and whose pronouncing was not to be encouraged, Leung was unmoved. "I have seen it," he lied, and turned to an editorial in *Figaro*.

"But but,—" pushed Barouche, "You do not take me seriously. I am telling you that you would adore it. Not just enjoy it. You must. It's not *The River*, you know. It's not *Le carrosse d'or*. But it's something. You should see it today."

"Yes," said Leung, really without the least interest.

"Because," said Barouche, "We never know what will happen tomorrow."

This last had the effect of a pinprick at the back of Leung's neck, because he was indeed a person who routinely considered the drawbacks of mortality. As he passed by the theater a little later, and looked at the posters tacked up beside the kiosk, he saw that the film was indeed *Le carrosse d'or*. "What's the matter with that Barouche," he said to himself, "that he cannot remember a title? He's dissipated. It's not so difficult a title to remember. I remember titles all the time. And besides, he always thinks he's smart." Leung paid for a ticket and went in to watch *Le carrosse d'or*, during which, as the case would have it, he fell asleep.

But people had been passing by and picking up syllables, as people will, and word got around that Barouche was dissipated. You'd never believe how many started turning away when he approached, heading off to the water cooler, finding on a high shelf a portfolio that suddenly needed re-reading. People returned his telephone calls, but only after an extensive delay. It was a sunny Saturday morning, and in the tiny park that margins the Saint Germain-des-Près, that he next had opportunity to corner Leung.

"I've decided I give too much advice," said he, twirling the end of his little beard. "What's your opinion? Do I give advice too much?" He giggled into Leung's face quite charmingly, or else with poisoned accusation: it was impossible to tell. But he didn't wait for an answer. "That's *my* estimation, at any rate, and from now on, you should stop listening to me."

[Lillebrød of the Golden Coach]

HEXXENDELSEN

arrived at fifteen minutes after four, as the sky was darkening toward the weekend, and occupied the territory for more than an hour and a half, leaning back in a rigid chair and explaining in rather more detail than had been requested the intricacies of the new budgetary scheme. Special attention was given the magnitude of the yearly gas bill, attributed in substantial part to the use on every floor below the seventeenth (where the executives had their own kitchens) of spontaneous heaters and cooking coils. Hexxendelsen had worked out protocols, and rather too many of them, in fact. And as he had trimmed his moustache rather too forcefully, revealing his hairlip, it was not an altogether pleasant duration as he explained them. You could see in the distance the silvery harbor, and with blue smoke a steamer was outbound for Alexandria. Hexxendelsen and the Executive Vice-President had rounded off an ancient plan to decentralize the finances, with the disastrous outcome that marketing operations from here to Rio de Janeiro were in serious jeopardy. In every department, secretaries were fuming. Disconcertion was everywhere: the departmental liaisons were lost in spreadsheets, and, rolling over with gastroenteritis imported from Macao, the agents assigned to escort visiting luminaries were in the thrall of nervous palpitations because a wire from the Barcelona office had inspired new bi-weekly reports.

He had been offered a cigar and now he was offered another, but Hexxendelsen sat and fidgeted. When finally he stood and walked out, it was as much as ten minutes before the realization struck him that he'd left his briefcase on the floor behind him. He said he'd much rather stop for a beer than flirt with all these prognostications, and indeed he was offered a beer, but "No no no no no," a little chirp, he had to get the six-eleven from Felstad, and he had a weekend of calculations looming ahead. "I'll be up all night in calculations," said he, "I'll be up all night." And he added, as though to an audience that hadn't quite grasped the enormity of what was to be grasped, "It's very complicated, and I can't explain." There was something sad hovering over his face, but Leung, trying to commiserate, found himself rebuffed by a great sternness, a dignity, a self-reliance that was all but offensive.

When he had his cubicle to himself again,

Leung picked up his telephone and dialed for his voicemail, three somber messages about contracts unfulfilled. There were more contracts to deal with than ever before, hundreds every day, and to his mind, which he would have admitted was romantic, they were—well, it hardly mattered what he thought, because his own contract made no provisions for the expression of opinion. If it was true that in the early years he had formed opinions and struggled to find avenues for making them public, these days no one had time for thinking things over. These days one stood and made faces in the elevator, one complained about the weather, one said one needed a holiday. It was amazing how many people lounged around the elevators complaining that they needed a holiday, especially after just returning from holidays. Everyone stood in the elevator and said, "I need a holiday more than I've ever needed a holiday in all my life. God, this place makes me need a holiday." No one, however, was going off on holiday, not any longer, or not now, not after the Big Memorandum, as it was lovingly called. Nothing after the Big Memorandum was the same. Leung stopped thinking of things to say to express his opinion. He developed an appetite and ate lunches out, started putting on weight.

At *Nobuhatsu*, on Berningsgade, the waitress delayed over the rice wine, he thought condescendingly, and the sushi were a little dry. Not a little dry, very dry. Stale. Unbelievable. She stood silent as an elm, trying to give the impression of trying to please. He finished his yam rolls and sat for a long time staring at the plate.

"We will have to enforce all clauses in the contract," read a note that arrived at 3 p.m. one afternoon soon later, after the New Year had begun and everyone had fallen into that bit of tranquil sadness. Senior managers started calling meetings and repeating the magical phrase, "Enforce all clauses." Huge proposals were prepared and circulated. A firm arrived from Hamburg and with great ladders encircled the building, replaced all the old windows with new ones that couldn't open. An air-heating and -conditioning system was installed, that hummed. A new telephone system was installed, to replace receptionists.

One by one, over the next several months, the old workers gave up, and with the comment, "I am tired of enforcing this lousy contract," retired from the company. One by one, they were replaced with brash youngsters who carried portfolios most energetically and murmured, "This contract is fascinating." A machine was installed in the lobby which whirred and had a circular prismatic device spinning in front of a grinding motor, and people walked past it without looking. Leung resigned and took a job driving a tram car up the Berulinius Hill.

It was about this time that Hexxendelsen came to the conclusion it would be better to operate without a contract, altogether. He put up a proposal, and it was cleared at the Board. He called people to meetings and had them draw up contingency plans for carrying on without a contract. "People will follow directives, or their paychecks will be canceled," he said. "It will be easier this way."

People came to follow directives, and no longer gathered near the elevators. And it was dismaying to see that no one worked with any energy or spark. "Our product," said Hexxendelsen, "sells around the world and we earn incalculable profit. We're doing brilliantly. Everyone should be enthusiastic." But no one had a spark of energy when he worked, and everyone followed directives, and the bank balance became fatter and fatter, as, in fact, did Hexxendelsen, who was soon promoted to a very high office with a window from which he could see only the clouds.

[Lillebrød of the Contract]

IN THE LITTLE VILLAGE

next to our village on the east side of the great inward Bay, there once lived an old lady who had four hairless dogs. They were not large, and they were colored dark as liver, and often they bared their teeth, so that there was an air of offensiveness and fear spread through the tiny population by these beasts.

"Like living pieces of sausage," the Major would sneer as the old lady walked the dogs in the morning along the waterfront. "Like giant rats. Like something out of a horrible nightmare." It was curious to imagine that the Major had nightmares like the rest of us.

Everyone knew that the old lady had very little money. She would sit tearing scraps off her hunk of meat to feed to the hairless dogs, so that finally she had very little left for herself. She sickened and died.

They came to clean out her house but no one could find the hairless dogs. "The dogs have run off," said the chief of police.

But not a soul had seen the hairless dogs go

running. And at night, people claimed, there was howling to be heard from the house where the old lady had been. The authorities came and nailed boards across all the windows and doors, because the old lady had left no children and consequently there was no one to inherit the property. The lawyers came and sat around a table and bared their teeth at one another and threw papers upon papers.

About a week later, someone said they had seen four hairless dogs roaming the cliffs that lay behind the village. These are called the Cliffs of Austerlitz, for the strange reason that on the second of December, 1805, at the same time as Napoléon's army was running over Alexander's in that celebrated battle, that is, not long after eight o'clock in the morning, a fault that had run the length of this rocky promontory for hundreds and hundreds of years suddenly split in the ferocious cold that came upon the area that winter, with the result that huge pieces of land fell off into the Bay, leaving the sheer drop that is still there now. People came to think it was the force of the Napoléonic personality that traveled through space and struck those rocks, or perhaps they simply adored the Emperor, but the Cliffs took on that reverberant name. The dogs, at any rate, had been spotted, and now it seemed that something had to be done.

The lawyers made an announcement. The old lady, whom everyone thought a pauper, had in truth been unbelievably rich, so much so that she was the owner of all the land on which the village stood. There was nothing she did not own, the Cliffs of Austerlitz included. And her holdings ran back for miles, including vast acreage adjacent to our own village. Needless to say, people were astounded. But the mayor, a toothless carpenter named Stenkt, made a very fine speech. "We must be respectful. The territory she owned is now in the province of the hairless dogs. As long as we continue to respect them, we may continue to live in this place."

And so it happened that people came to lay out food, day and night, for the hairless dogs, and the food having disappeared they laid out more and more. People said, once in a while, that they had seen a hairless dog or two disappearing under a fence, into a woods, or between two old buildings covered with tarpaper. The howling ceased.

[Lillebrød of the Hairless Dogs]

HAVING DRILLED INTO

the largest vault in the largest bank in the largest city of our country, a man stole off with hundreds of billions of gølder in a big satchel. He drove silently to the airport, armed with a gun, and hijacked a jet aircraft that was bound by the northern route for Tokyo.

Somewhere over our territory, however, this crazy desperado, having laced himself into a parachute and having forced the chief stewardess at gunpoint, a woman from Tampere named Bettet, to assist him, caused the emergency rear exit to be opened (at notable danger to everyone on board) and dropped himself into the sky. "What a daring idea," said the agents at Interpol, "to imitate D. B. Cooper!" They had already planned to have a small army waiting for him when the plane landed, and saw now with chagrin that he would surely escape the hands of justice.

But it happened that his parachute failed to open. Hours afterward, in the mountainous district of Urho Kekkosen, nearby our tiny hamlet named Tyttor, not far from Laanila (as it is now called; it was formerly Bsøwet), his body was found in a spruce forest by two boys with their dogs. The satchel of money, however, was not by his side.

It need hardly be said that there was enough cash to keep whole villages alive for decades, or that the hills around Tyttor were jammed overnight with hunters and scavengers of all ages. All the way from Helsinki, and even across the borders from Norway and Sweden, came prospectors, and also enterprising sellers of hot food and blankets with colorful little caravans which they set up to resemble a carnival. Portable toilets, portable showers, portable living quarters appeared on wheels, and the forest rangers appeared in their tan and maroon uniforms, and the agents of the government appeared with their spectacles. Hundreds of television journalists materialized out of thin air, from every continent, with their transmission trucks and dressing rooms and phalanxes of assistants. The Holy Synod of Finland actually sent down a portable church, and within two days, two men from Blytyt—a village in the hills of which they constituted together twenty percent of the population—arranged to have a swimming pool dug and put up signs, SHOWER BEFORE ENTERING.

The old people of the precinct sat and smoked

and knitted and told stories of old times. When they saw all the newcomers they smiled and said to one another, "Winter will come before spring. Spring will come before summer. At summer's end, we will see the aurora borealis."

Many rumors circulated about the exact number of gølder in the missing satchel, and after the fourteenth day, when the robber was buried in a ceremony that very few attended, the rumors expanded and the number of gølder tripled. Some even hypothesized that he had secreted the money on his person somehow, and so with remarkable speed the grave was dug up and the coffin opened for a search. But still the hijacker lay dead and there was not a farthing to be seen.

The Minister of the Interior and the Chancellor of the Exchequer were quite concerned together about the effect of a loss of so much cash on the value of our currency, and in a weak moment the former said something to this effect to an editorialist from the Helsinki Grand Press who had a symphonic style and an ear for scaremongering. (The Prime Minister's press secretary went snow white when he heard about this, but what could he do?) The Chancellor babbled demurrals but no one ever listens to him. What an editorial was composed, in tones as gray as thunderclouds! The market subsequently fell. In the smaller cities, such as Krounst and Vanninlen, the bourgeois owners of dress shops and theaters saw in their imaginations gold-ribboned packages of investments plummeting to earth like robbers from the sky. This vision made them go gray and rush to sell, with the result that stocks did indeed catapult; and now, rendered destitute by the failure of the exchange, these pillars of society ran on their own behalves to search for buried gølder in the Kekkonen hills; and hastened to put up around their digs barbed wire fences along which vicious Pinschers prowled on long leash.

The old people of Tyttor and Laanila sat and smoked and knitted and told stories of old times. When they saw the vicious dogs and the purring limousines, they smiled to one another and said, "Winter will come before spring. Spring will come before summer. At summer's end the aurora borealis will shine in our sky."

Depressurized by its open rear door, the aircraft in question had itself been forced to make an emergency landing at Murmansk. Here the traumatized Bettet was removed to hospital and the rear door mechanism was repaired. After only an hour and a half—an astonishing record—the flight was able to depart once again for Tokyo, with a fresh crew and free drinks for every passenger.

One customer needed no whiskey, however. The individual who had been seated next to the robber was a Dr Kings-Whyte from the United Kingdom, actually from the Department of Philosophy at the University of Saint Andrews. Before the original take-off, he had administered himself a sleeping pill, so that all through the escapade with the parachute escape, and all through the emergency landing at Murmansk, and even well into the recommencement of the flight he had been soundly ensconced in dreamland. He awoke over Siberia to find the seat next to him empty but the satchel that his companion had curiously entrusted to him still safe beneath his own seat. The stranger must be in the lavatory, he told himself. Or else he had migrated to another row where on a trio of empty seats it would be possible to spread oneself for a decent night's sleep on the long flight.

Not that even large aircraft like this one make it possible to get a sound sleep. But whatever.

With these half-thoughts, the thinker fell back into a dream himself.

It was one of those very powerful sleeps which

overtake us when we are happiest, or when we
see nothing of our future. Dr Kings-Whyte did
not awaken until the flight had been standing for
twenty minutes or more at the gate in Tokyo and,
with an eager bustle, the tired stewards were hur-
rying stragglers off the plane. In his half daze, the
motion of the uniformed stewards back and forth
up the empty aisle was surreal and pleasant—sug-
gestive of some phrases of Parmenides, actually. He
could see through his porthole that outside it was
pouring rain, and horrible flashes of lightning were
lighting up the tarmac blue and violet. Quickly as
he could, being still unawake, the man stood, gathered his coat and hat and newspaper, and allowed
himself to be guided down the aisle and into the
terminal building with a worrying thought that
perhaps the Japanese customs officials didn't speak
English and he didn't know how to say "academic
conference" in Japanese.

Only when he was safe in his taxi, speeding into
the rain, did he recall the satchel he had left beneath the seat. He told himself, "The fellow came
back and took it before I awoke. And if not, the
men who clean the airplane will take care of it."

Because the airplane had been diverted to Russia, and because the hijacker had jumped in mid-

flight, the authorities had not bothered to indicate to the ground crew in Tokyo that there was anything special about this flight. The team that did come on to clean the plane, therefore, all covered in neon lime green vests, and who with great green plastic bags swallowed up everything the two hundred and fourteen passengers had left behind, Kleenex, paper cups, forty pairs of headphones, chewing gum, receipts, torn tickets, a satchel, three t-shirts, seventeen wrappers from chocolate bars, and much more, were so tired and bored, with another seventeen flights ahead of them before they could tumble home to bed. They worked in a mechanical flurry, tossing all their garbage bags into a great blue garbage dumpster that was picked up in the morning by a great blue truck and hauled to an incineration site behind a great blue sign in Urawa, where all of it was burned to cinders.

What was the robber's plan in leaving that bag with his neighbor, and in neglecting to bring it off the plane? No one will ever know, and more pertinently: no one will ever ask.

Flashy billboards now went up outside the hamlet of Tyttor: "TREASURE BURIED HERE . . . A GREAT PLACE TO RAISE A FAMILY."

The mayor was accused by a lawyer and a veterinarian of having found the money and of having sent it off secretly to a bank account in Switzerland. He denied it vehemently. For benefit of a newspaper photographer, his wife and daughter cried. The photographer, to give him credit, produced an estimable rendering of a pathetic family scene. But the veterinarian, a harsh man from Germany, brought a character witness—a waitress who, it seems, had had an affaire de coeur with the mayor ten years earlier, and who had been left by him with child—and the mayor's credibility was summarily impeached. The veterinarian went further and made a speech at our town hall. "The reprehensible moral culpability of government . . . a liar and a reprobate . . . turning our charming homes into a commercial free-for-all, and pocketing all the licence money . . ."

"Get out of town!" called Ritili, the man who owned the gas station.

"Go away!" called Madame Lemite, the woman who owned the restaurant.

"Unholy pig!" cried Torne, the fourth-grade teacher.

The mayor packed up his family and moved away.

The old people sat and smoked and knitted and

told stories of old times. When they heard the rumors about the mayor they smiled at one another and said, "Winter will come before spring. Spring will come before summer."

Now that the mayor was gone—Filthy Frasca, people called him behind his back—the veterinarian charged that it had been Aarlen the lawyer who had found the money and sent it off to Switzerland, and that he had been in collusion, Aarlen, with that despicable personage and rotten excuse for a public servant, Filthy Frasca. The lawyer sued the veterinarian for defamation and the case dragged on for many years, during which time poor old Frasca died and the many ramshackle business ventures that had sprung to life around the treasure hunt became established and entrenched in the economic life of our hamlet. In place of the portable toilets and sleeping quarters, for example, was the plush new Treasure Trove Hotel. In place of the coffee wagons and fast food trucks was a trio of restaurants. So protracted were the legal proceedings, in fact, that the owner of the hotel put up a new wing before the verdict was handed down.

The old people sat and smoked and knitted and told stories of old times.

The veterinarian, Lachtner, was found guilty.

All of the population of Tyttor had been divided by this case, and now half the people, the ones who had supported Aarlen the lawyer, resented the others, who had supported Lachtner the veterinarian, and held meetings in order to express this resentment and to help it grow. They became, first, angry; and then outraged; and then livid. "All Germans are alike . . ." Many pulled their money out of the bank and their children out of the school. "A village taken over by Germans . . ." Soon, it seemed the school would have to close. The bank merged with another, in Laanila, but some officers in the Laanila bank mishandled some funds very badly so that within a year both banks crumbled into file folders in the State Receiver's office. Without the help of the bank, the Treasure Trove Hotel couldn't pay its construction bills, so it closed and one saw yellow boards tacked over the windows where once gay little rows of nasturtiums had bloomed. Now with fewer than half the number of hungry people to feed each night, all of the restaurants went out of business except one, a pancake house, and this was open only on Saturdays. And after some months, people got tired of pancakes. Tyttor became a ghost town. The paint on the billboards—TREASURE BURIED HERE . . . A GREAT PLACE

TO RAISE A FAMILY—faded and chipped.

The old people of our hamlet sat and smoked and told of old times, peaceably, as old people will do when battles are over. Winter would be followed by spring and spring would be followed by summer, they knew, and the birds that had flown south would return. When you told a stranger the story of the missing satchel with the great fortune inside, the stranger would stop, as sure as shooting, and wonder if this was a place to set up camp, for never was there a stranger who didn't think, "No matter who has searched for that money, surely I am the one who will find it." At night the old people walked to the edge of town and saw the aurora borealis light up the sky.

[Lillebrød of the Falling Man]

Dream with Caillebotte

GÉVIGNE WAS ALWAYS TO BE FOUND MASTERING

one of those windowed prospects that open out onto the great Boulevards, standing through his afternoons while the sunlight capped his shoulders with golden trapezia, a cigar gone cold in his mouth, and his gaze fixed like an artilleryman's upon the movements of the shivering crowd. Where the Boulevard Haussmann intersects the rue Lafayette he gazed out; and where the Avenue Wagram is cut by the rue de Courcelles, etc. There was a most delicious sense of being trapped in an engagement, of being framed squarely in the middle of a complicated happening the motive for which need never—because it lay in the most obscure blurs of the past—be discovered nor its outcome with any accuracy predicted, so long as the rhythms and colors, the perfumes accenting the gestures and exasperations, might be drunk to the full. If he had been trained for banking, and if it was true that a million and a half passed through his hands upon a random lunch hour, nevertheless mechanical thoughts and diligent pursuits did not

lure him, and gave him no sense of pleasure or measure of contentment, if they offered to his greater
sensibilities no opportunity of melding a perception with a plan; a glimpse with an explication; fla-
vors with rationales; and shapes, bulk, the bristle of
corporeality, the delicate suggestion of movement
unresolved, the happy burden of timbre with cali-
bration, weight, estimation, and therefore value.
His life was therefore given out in a kind of warm
pool of sensation and artifice, calculus and dream.
As he sat reading his newspaper near the balcony
across from the Winterburg, it was the penum-
brous violet velvet of his sister's gown, as she stood
next to him gazing into the street, that captured his
attention, not the quotation upon iron shares that
rested, or rather palpitated, before his eyes. He felt
calm in the assurance that to have begun in the
middle this way, to have begun one's sensation and
one's story, was to admit of a certain acquiescence,
a calming surrender, and to know, with some bliss-
ful surety, that resolution was safely out of the
question. Like a mollusc, he lived within the history of his own excrescence, since the delights and
the sensations that filled him had been projected
upon their referents—out there, outside the window—this was most clear—by himself. He was

holding a little book by Vicomte de l'Îsle Adam, with a citron cover, into which he had plunged, as a desperate sponge diver might, deeply and without concern for orderliness. He was in the middle, had begun in the middle, would swirl around there, with a little Armagnac, and not permit himself to escape, nor would he permit himself the cold sharp feeling of awakeness that could force him to a regularity instead of a comfortable middling. The middle was a world, simply and utterly, the world that was presently his universe, and Lisette, for all her modesties, had surely entered it and set upon the dining table, at some moment outside his observations and therefore perfectly, plates with oranges and knives, and goblets of crystal, and a cake made from plums. Her fiancé, to whom she had been introduced by the somewhat despicable Eugène Dufresne, of all people, would join them soon, or so she said, and the cake had been made big enough in case others arrived as well, his mother, for instance, although this was unlikely enough. This young paragon, at any rate—she called him this!—went by the name of Léopold de Brasseur, and stood out in a room for the definitiveness with which he asked far too pertinent questions, the defiance with which he carted the blackest intention and devotion into what was otherwise a kind of lambent cocoon of tranquil impersonability. It may well have been the cocaine or the absinthe that made things seem so vital as long as they were abstract and impertinent—this was surely Dufresne's rather haughty opinion—but it made little sense to think of pinning causes to substances since, first, there was no organized knowledge in the matter and, then, since, as he had no intention of disabusing himself of these charms these scandalous attributions of effect could only be considered moot. Dufresne was, for example, by no means a reader, and had probably turned the first page of his own pristine copy of that Adam before he had turned the second, in an insensate disregard for the— there was no other word for it—flesh of the thing. One had to open with lust, or at least with terror; but one did not proceed to a bound volume as though it called for a military plan of attack. Brasseur's, at any rate, was not the figure that presented itself in Gévigne's doorway after an importunate pounding. It was a telegraph, demanding his immediate attentions in the apartment of an old widow on the sixth floor of a building on the rue Halévy, to which dismal and rather waxen locale he repaired himself without delay—or without, it can be said, undue delay, since he did stop a little out of the way for some crêpes framboise on the rue de Mogador (an entertainment that, no matter what else may be said, was suitable for a man of his position and reputation). It was a matter of providing some predictions of the movement of oil shares, and the old lady was happy to provide a nice tisane and some cold fricassée. Again he fell into the deliquescent swoon of the dreamer, catching his eye upon the tapestries with which she had caused her armchairs to be upholstered. Her voice, questioning, indeed, was a song for him, though he had not the slightest idea of who she was or what she intended to do with the information he provided. It began to drizzle, and the clock struck two o'clock of the afternoon. "Je pourrai vous dire maintenant," said she, rather harshly, it seemed, as a way of addressing a total stranger, "que j'intend à vous procurer pendant une heure et demi, et si l'on trouve après cette reservation qu'il pleurait beaucoup plus fort, s'il s'agirait d'une deluge, j'avoue que je n'aurais aucun acceuil sous mon toit gentil jusqu'au bout." He scarcely paid attention to this, but she did insist on continuing, with a little rap of her stick on the newly stripped parquet as she paced back and forth, "Parce que les hommes en general,

dire les êtres masculins, m'ont trouble affreuse-
ment, m'ont gaché, tant qu'il m'est necessaire de me
protéger un peu, enfin." He took himself, a little
saddened, back to the rue de Mogador and found
Estienne Givray making the rounds of the cafés in
search of an afternoon's respite, but rien. The men
who sat with menthes and silk hats enshadowing
their bearded faces were pompous types, men of
the market, no doubt, and pointed at their newspapers authoritatively as they challenged one another
across the rickety little tables. Gévigne thought it
would be delicious, indeed, if he could be rid of
Givray and could travel the boulevard, now glistening and enflavored from the rain, in the company of a delicious female in pearl earrings, whose
dress would be lined with fur, and who would take
delight in gliding beside him and taking shelter
from his umbrella. The light was failing now, and
the shadows, such as there were, had taken on a cast
of violet, but Gévigne did not flag and wept, as he
walked, at the beauty of the unrelenting presence
of it all. A man dragged by with a cart heavy with
tomatoes. It was unlikely, Gévigne knew, that he
would sleep tonight, and he promised himself to
come into possession of a little notebook in which
it would be possible to make drawings and little

inscriptions, a kind of catalogue without end and without beginning. But now, as he stood in a tiny shop fronted with green on the rue Saint-André-des-Arts, very near the rue des Grands Augustins, picking through notebooks, M. G. Caillebotte walked through the door and caught sight of him, eagerly. "Mon très cher monsieur," the painter began, in a voice as soothing as ferns, "What I would not give for a gentleman such as yourself, embroiled as he must be in the misgivings and adventures of everyday life, to withdraw voluntarily into the cooling reservation of my gaze. Bring yourself, I humbly entreat, to my studio at 31, Boulevard Haussmann, and allow me to transfigure you into an illumination! You will pose for me, and I will cause de l'hommard and des écrivisses to be served to you on a great brass platter. I will cause a timbale d'épinards, a gratin, de la truite en gêlée, all of this to be yours. I will set at your feet a group of musicians to perform Haydn or, better even, Scarlatti. Come to my studio, cher monsieur." And so on. Gévigne permitted a calèche to be sent for. He stopped and refreshed himself, changed cravats, adorned his coat with a selection from the florist in the rue Lafitte, that charming but utterly preoccupied lady with the pencil behind her ear and the handful of green wires, now binding roses to carnations, carnelians, sprigs of berry. There was such a flurry in those days, the wagons speeding down the street at a notable clip, students throwing themselves upon one another as they raced down the sidewalk to the Librairie d'Antan, a gaunt little buffon standing on the corner waving colored bladders in the air. This Madame Leyriffe, for that was her name, had been in the process of instructing a young gentleman on the fine points of the cultivated dahlia, but now she interrupted herself and selected a pink rose to affix to Gévigne, giving him at no charge a little dispensation, "Tiens, you should not fail to vote in the election tomorrow, your type is always neglecting its civic responsibility, is this not so?" The painter's studio at 31, Boulevard Haussmann was a very high room, with yellowing mirror all along one side and a great porte dorée giving onto the wide prospect of the busy avenue. Upon the little balcony outside, Gévigne positioned himself, his hat pulled low over his face so that the great Nadar, should he brush past under a cloud in that hot air balloon of his, would be afforded no unrecompensed view of his expressions. These expressions, indeed, were no longer of hunger or satiation, or delight or discomfort, or confusion, but had passed into a delirium of anxiousness and despair, in equal admixture, with the result that Gévigne rocked forward against the balustrade and then drew himself back into the great room, his head aching and his coat feeling close. He tore it off. "It may be," said Caillebotte, with his little lisp, "that you and I will develop a kinship of the soul. I will know the petty details of your life and you will divine every aspect of my vision of you, so that in the end I may have your license to follow and illustrate all those delicious confusions which enchain themselves to form your existence, and you, for your part, may come to reside with contentment and perhaps even a little good humor within the strictures of my gaze." Caillebotte's canvas came to seem for Gévigne nothing less than a hearth, in fact, from which blew up into the air all the sparks of his own existence. It was as though all of the earth swirled in a vortex around the easel of Caillebotte, and here the man worked like a very fiend, his eyes first glowing like coals, then yellowing like a cat's, and finally graying and remaining opaque; his nourishment—delivered by a maid with a limp—left uneaten upon the little bamboo table; the daylight thinning until it seemed one would choke on the darkness; and the street be-

coming enfogged; and messages coming by the
hour to which Caillebotte gave spitting incoherent
responses; and the word Degas uttered with con-
tempt; and the chain of canvases seeming to be
endless; and the reptilian light; Gévigne's hair; a
wordrobe being brought in by a young assistant
dressed all in black, with his hair reeking of gen-
tian; the curtains drawn aside; the sound of a jeer-
ing crowd coming from the direction of the Opéra;
Caillebotte cursing and arranging oranges upon a
compote; petits four being sent up from the Place
de la Madeleine; a hundred girls sneaking into
Caillebotte's bedchamber; Gévigne's legs tortured
with pain. Caillebotte had a monstrous mask from
central Africa, the teeth made of cowrie shells and
the eyes daubed with red paint. Everything here
was like a waking dream, and as the days proceeded
and Gévigne caught sleep in shards, his dreams
took on a clarity and sensibility and became realer,
so that soon, late in the morning when the absinthe
had been consumed, it became impossible to be
certain whether one was sleeping or awake, and
Caillebotte moved around with his brushes, like a
satyr. I should write, perhaps, "And now, without
warning, a letter arrived that changed everything."
Or better, "And this continued until a certain

morning, when—." Yet, although life seemed to lose its edge and the colors of objects gradually melted together into something quite beyond description, nothing so dramatic as this did occur to Gévigne as he was replaced on canvas by Caillebotte. For art, at least the art of Caillebotte, was an organ of life and not a vehicle speeding through it, and this was why his canvases alarmed the critics so. He had found a way even without the aperture of the camera to bound and sever life in slices, tranches as the charcutier said, thin and delicate as the slices of truffle with which one bejeweled one's crème de choufleur, or at least this was distinctly the way it seemed when one caught the chilling aura of human society subjected to a dispensation and an abstraction. The critics hated it, and said so, and complained, and yet he painted, and he followed Gévigne and painted him three times a week at least. Nevertheless, a certain morning did come at the culmination of which—

LIKE A MOLLUSC,

he lived within the history of his own excrescence, so that now, to touch the world, he was forced to erode a pathway diligently, by means of the tiniest abrasions mounted upon one another in a great panoply of dedication, and he had to prevent himself, indeed, from crying, lest the tears themselves harden to thwart him. He could see that all his life he had been taunted by fabrications impossible to believe, that the war, for example, was, as everyone claimed, the crux of his civilization (when he had no trouble seeing that in fact it had been merely a press conference interrupted by fragments of film clips: green fireworks, a zoom shot of a warehouse, a man caressing the nose of his aircraft as though it belonged to a favorite horse). He was aware that he spent the greater part of his time in conversation with those who did not understand him, and had, indeed, made the ambiguity of such a confounding situation a source of pleasure and a condition for repose. His oldest friends refused to speak with him. The healing still incomplete, and threatening for some time to remain so, he was in no position to gauge his condition, and so it was quite impossible for him to be sure it was not merely the lapse of time itself that had rendered him so generally incapable, but he did wonder if when he emerged he would be as fresh as ever or else gored by that metaphysical bull that had come to be waiting outside, that beast of complete and unrelenting negativity. A nice piece of roast pork would be mere cholesterol; a walk through the spring forest, its floor dappled with many-colored primula, an invitation to become lost among clusters of poisonous mushrooms; that worn book of poems, Lopez de Vega de Vega's *Cataclysms in a Jar*, no longer a fountainhead but only a publisher's bait, bound, indeed, with toxic glue; the charming students he encountered Tuesday nights in the gorgeous salon of Prof. Balmian-Sevigny only cupidinous mutants, love suckers in love with themselves; the adorable project of building a desk for himself nothing but a defeat in the making, since he knew nothing of wood or blades, and even the briefest imagination of sunlight beaming upon rosewood focused his attention on the thousands of pages of manuscript that would be jumbled in chaos there. Although he had the vague sense, and unmistakably, that the world accepted him as a kind of entertainment or comestible, it was true as well that through his protective shield events could inject no pleasure, and so he labored on in a blind and rarified faith that one morning he would wake happily and the warm air would caress his cheek. He fell without warning into fits of profound slumber, dreamless, black, and wakened always to queries, glances, troubling encryptions. He telephoned Garofalo. "My book," said this one, "has finally come! And the Kokosch has come! And the Fantini has come, too! And it was my birthday! And I am unloading boxes." Garofalo had been in New York, Chicago, Buenos Aires, Houston, Miami, Paterson, New Jersey, and San Francisco. "I ate in some wonderful restaurants." A good meal was a sure prelude to gas. He covered his eyes and turned on the radio. They were still babbling about the war, that myth, that collective dream, or more accurately, that lagoon which was dream in the precincts where he floated. They said that thousands had been killed and he told himself, "On the other side of the lagoon, no doubt," but it was a challenge to believe the lagoon had another side far away from the stories and fragments of story that came into his ears. He told himself that logically there must be another side of the lagoon, there must be suffering, people starved and were tortured, and suddenly the image came into his mind of Theissen, that old irritant, that spore, who had said, finally, "This is a lagoon. There is another side to it. There is suffering, there is torture. I am going to the other side to cure the world. Come with me." But he knew there was no cure. No cure at all. Theissen telephoned once or twice over the years, regaling him with accounts of his many adventures in the war, and the truth was (he had to admit this), Theissen made him feel ashamed for having resided in his hardened imaginations, and ashamed for having committed himself, in a time of bullets, to text, and so he sent a little money to an address Theissen gave, but it became clear that sending money was only another imagination, and then one day Theissen stopped calling. Once, years afterward, Theissen sent a Hallmark card showing a little church in the snow, that read, "In a world of poverty and pain, art is unimportant." Now the engines were throbbing, as though someone had called for increased speed, and he recollected that this same Theissen who belittled him for having made no contribution, had sent his own children into the war. It was far better to send one's own children into peace, even, and especially, if it were a peace of one's own making. The engines began

to whine. It was curious to have a distinct sense of
motion but no sense of where one was going, and
he realized that this—this innocence—was not
Theissen's perception of life at all, Theissen always
saw the road ahead, if only for a limited distance,
and that was a different way of being, to be sure, if
not a crippling disaster. Here in the warmth of the
placid part of the lagoon the critical distinctions
were smaller, distinguished by nuance, no less a
part of the great architecture for one's inability to
place them upon a blueprint, and the voice, one's
voice, that voice one knew as one's own was everything, surely, at least everything he possessed that
could be used in this place, that magnified and silent voice, and the murmurings and harmonies of
it, the rocky elisions and amphibious metaphors,
its unspelled images and promontories of feeling
must, too, constitute a life. In the riddle of the
argument or the song, he had chosen the song. A
musky odor was on his hands, bringing up the smell
of grapes and sweet firewood a long time back, almost back at the beginning, and the whistling winter wind locked out, cold blue daylight blanketing
the pantry, the black grapes piled in wooden crates
high over the sweet firewood, and he was collaps-
ing in the smell of it, and grandmother was making

tea. Shockingly then, and as though it were present again, he recollected his first sex, the other mouth encroaching upon his ear, the tongue entering, and he knew that sounds were coming out of him, and he heard himself crying, and awoke.

AND WHAT IF I SHOULD ASK THIS QUESTION,

whether it is the case that in wearing this robe and sitting to write by this candlelight I may be considered to be enrobed and candlelit? Or whether instead, with the robe clinging to my shoulders, it can be said only that I am, that I exist, and that a condition of enrobedness is attached to me under circumstances that can be specified and that are ultimately cultural, aesthetic, economic, but not essential, and that in my essential state I am, therefore, indeed indescribable. What if I should ask about the storks that hover over the city, resting upon the chimneytops? What if M. Bernardin, Chef de la Préfecture de Police, arrives in his cape and announces that changes are about to take place, and that I am to head a committee to oversee them in every detail? As I can see only the cravat, the silk shirt, the cape, what is M. Bernardin except a certain manifestation of gestures, one following the other in a ceaseless seamless flow? Gouvot the barber has waxed Bernardin's moustache and curled up the corners in a profound statement of the resonance and perduration of the XIXème siècle. Yellow roses are set in a vase with mimosa. We must travel to purchase a small quantity of flour and some raisins, raisins that live temporarily in a brown paper bag, and then we must swiftly return in the chilling wind that is anticipating snow. We move through an alley next to a shack covered with brick-colored tarpaper and smelling of fried onions. The ground is hard as rock. At the railway track we smell diesel fuel and rusting iron in the cold air. Grandmother bakes raisin buns. Bernardin has twice been divorced, and there are stories about cruelty and about children. A woman who travels to the city to work in the Pigalle shares his house. Her name is Lavette. Grandmother says she is low. Bernardin is always very dignified with her. What if I should ask, is this the light of a candle or is this the light of God conveyed in this instance by a candle? Is this permeating light or rebounding light, as it strikes this arm of mine, and what gives me to think the arm is my arm, or that it is an arm, and how do I call this light? As I sit enrobed by this candlelight, how may I pronounce upon the moral status of Bernardin as he escorts Lavette out of his house, turns on the walk, moves to the limit of my perception and crosses the limit of the horizon, disappears? I am sent to purchase a bag of raisins. I recollect the dark nutty confines of the provisioner, the hand extending from beside the cash register, the sound of muttering. What if I should ask, what is recollection? What if I should ask, what is it that I recollect, an event or an account of an event? What if I should ask, what is a raisin? Is it not dried in the sun, is it not a recollection of the light of God? I can hear Lavette when she goes off in the morning, "Au revoir, au revoir. Non, non, je ne peux pas. Je ne peux pas. Au revoir. Je t'aime . . . !"

CAILLEBOTTE HAD NO IDEA WHAT TO

paint. He spent the long afternoon staring at his easel. The sun was obscured. A letter from Adel Gévigne sat unopened on the table, which had been polished with lime oil. In every direction, both in his sweet-smelling room and in the yard he could see through his large double windows, light was breaking itself into fragments and striking him with pungency, and color was ineffable, but he found himself unable to collect a vision. In his dream, he had been walking along a river in Johannesburg, one that split into canals running into and between the beautifully architected houses, and he climbed stone stairways and found himself with her, marveling at rooms painted green. She kissed him. "Look!" he whispered. Then at a doorway a woman presented herself, smiling with kindness and perplexity, and he realized they had somehow stepped into her home, that the pathway had led them into her salon, and he apologized and she showed them the door. He tried his hand at a self-portrait, eschewing the mirror this time, and found that the face he knew so well now shifted in his hands and became a landscape wracked by a turbulent storm. The lips curled in anger. The eyes seemed brilliant, yet also blind. Almost a century later, critics would compare this image to another self-portrait, painted in 1855 by his own master, Léon Bonnat. But Bonnat had been destitute at that time, had given up hope, while he, Caillebotte, wanted only, and with a hunger that was painful, to find an object. And they would say of him, too, how strange it was that he made his shadows violet, which was true, but as though shadows could be any other color. How strange it was that violet was in the shadows of Caillebotte. And now, looking at this canvas, he put more shadow in the eyes, violet, and glanced down at his arm to see what color jacket he was wearing, and De la Fresnaye sent word by a courier that there was great need of him at six at the Café des Deux Magots, so he finished up, and began to walk, and felt desperately thirsty. There was a decent little place in the rue Castiglione and he took an absinthe. This didn't help. It was nearing five-thirty. He asked for something by way of an eau de vie and the barman reached up and poured a colorless little glass of something that could have been raspberry, or pruneaux. There was very little time. Flurries had been blowing down for half an hour already. He entered the Tuileries at a quarter to six, knowing he would never make it on time, and had thoughts of darkness as he passed behind the Orangerie. The Pont de Solférino was dark, and a great wind had arisen, and the river was as black as coal, and as he walked he knew time was slowing and he would never make it, his hand white upon the balustrade, and there was suddenly a violet river smell, and he felt himself go down to his knees. This was it, he thought, and with a monstrous swish he heard a barge glide underneath him and felt himself as light as a feather descending. This was where they found him, his eyes open.

Dream of High Blood Pressure

Translated from the Polish,
"Sen z wysokie cisnienie"
by Wladyk Bol

WAYLAID

again in the vast autumnal forest, the courier arrived too late. The carriages raced and rattled upon the carpet of leaves, under the chartreuse trees which receded in the sweet chartreuse light, and the courier was outrun, halted, obliged to dismount, lashed to a tree trunk, blindfolded, branded upon his shoulder, PARTÚ. The Marquis had gone out at five. The château was empty and shortly after arriving there the carriages swept around in an oblong and then drew away in haste, the horses glistening under the black clouds. A breeze tickled the hazelnut trees that clustered at the margins of the great forest. How sad and beautiful are hazelnut trees in the autumn, their fruit browning and their branches tickled by the wind. A woman in the second carriage wore dark green velvet and the carriages rattled the leaves, monstrous piles of leaves. The king's seizures came and went unpredictably. The lovers stood in the deserted room, a dank room, its walls laid with tapestries, courting one another with glances, "Is it love?" Terrific bouquets spangled the corridor. Blinding light shone through high windows. One caught one's breath, as though trapped in a sequence of brave arpeggios. He repeated his mother's questions and she held her breath before replying softly, "The Marquis went out at five." He missed the clash of steel doors. "Why," she said, "were we born so hopeful and yet so hapless?" It became possible to think there would come a time when sensations would rush like comets, banishing reflection to the outer rim of a universe. The carriages racing through the forest stopped for nothing.

THE SHOOTING SHERRY

threw him into a light sleep and when he awoke in a daze he opened *The Seagull*, which he had been straining his eyes reading and found this: "I notice that cloud up there, shaped like a grand piano, and I make a mental note to put that in a story. 'A cloud passed, shaped like a grand piano.'" Putting the book in his lap he gazed out to the parterres through the beveled window glass, and a cloud passed, shaped like a grand piano.

THE FACT

of social pressure is undeniable. The teeth of the lion in the tapestry were blunted, but the leaves of the fig tree were sharp as razors. There are dynamisms evoked by emergency situations in life, early and late. Pastafaggiola boiled slowly in a great copper cauldron and all the high kitchen windows were opened to admit the sunlight. The Marquis had departed at five. He had left behind him, memoranda. The fact of social pressure is undeniable. The fact, the fact of pressure, the great fact, the impression of the fact, of the great impressive fact, the presence of the impression. The teeth of the lion in the tapestry were blunted, but the leaves of the fig tree were sharp as razors. Tiny needles and reddened fingers, sad maidens banished to the drawing room. The tea had been overbrewed. Mathilda von Mecklendorf-Bingen sat coyly. She ruffled the cuffs of her claret morning dress, and knew that her fingers were dry. A terrible dryness, at the tips of her fingers. Her thoughts could be understood metaphorically as a quilt. Her quilted thoughts overtook her. Revolving, but not neatly, and dropping. The Marquis, making his swift departure, had left behind him memoranda which were difficult to read. "My dear Mecky, in the matter of your estimable daughter, . . ." and so on. My dear, you are dear and I possess you, your dearness is to me, in my eyes you are great, you occupy a central space, the fountain springs from you and the garden girdles your waist. In the garden, mosquitoes replicated. She realized with a start that she had been presenting herself to him as a conundrum.

MEN RODE

after the carriages on sweating steeds, throwing up golden leaves, flashing swords. Or spears? Swords or spears, which? Knives? Daggers? Flashing daggers? Flashing blades? Men with great purple plumes in their hats rode after the carriages through the forest in the chartreuse light, shouting hoarsely, "The King!" What do we imagine to ourselves such men could have wished? To surround the royal carriage with torches and brilliant flashing teeth, to call out, "Long life to the King!" Perhaps it was their intention to kill the King. The King had done nothing to benefit anyone but His Royal Person and there was now much starvation and sickness. The rich nobles all had high blood pressure, suffered indigestion, had gout, were going blind. The Baron Byck was kept in darkness, swaddled in moist clothes. The Duke of Wagrowiec and Rogozno had inflammation of the kidneys and was fed dungwort tea, twelve glasses a day. The King was in the south of France. High blood pressure was everywhere, people had remorse, you couldn't find a soul who wasn't in the habit of chewing the leaves of the wild valerian, excellent against palpitations. You went into the higher heaths and looked for the telltale purple flowers, early in June, and while many boiled the root, it was a source of pleasure to masticate the lengthy winged leaves. The farmers of Kalisz kept their health, laboring in the swampy fields filled with mosquitoes, but had no food. The farmers of Gniezno, meanwhile, whose fields were owned directly by the King, waited through the long drought, then loaded their carts with hops and rye and drove them into the city, with but little hope. There were documents one had to carry, these had to be prepared at great cost by legal specialists. The boys of Grozdy, whose fathers were in the mercantile class, had plenty of leisure, and spent their afternoons practicing swordplay in the neighborhood of the game preserve of the forest lake of Prymzwiec, where the great gray herons fed. But they feared authority, and fled when the sheriff's men came to count the deer for the King. Near the river that ran at the bottom of the hill behind the great château, there was an old stone hut, used as a granary, and here during a thunderstorm the lovers met and lay together while the soldiers hunted for the girl. The smell of rye. The smell of rye.

THE MARQUIS WENT OUT

at five. This thought has already been expressed. I am speaking at present solely of our childhood. The courier arrived too late. "Ha, ha, three times done!" cackled the old witch-lady, czarownica. For a jolt to the system, try reading this aloud. He was helpless, but worse than helpless he was miserable. As early as 1793, the French were utilizing balloons for military purposes. The lovers stood in the deserted room while the soldiers searched for the girl. A blinding light shone through the curtains. "Mais enfin, shérif," insisted Passegrain, "je ne vois rien." I am speaking only of our childhood. There was a pond at the château and in it were dozens of golden carp and great sharp rocks mossed over. He was helpless, but worse than helpless he had the hunger and he was miserable.

A LION

will eat a truly large meal when it has the opportunity to do so. I turn to the operational record. I put to you the facts. Bessa came down for the weekend, with all her entourage and the copper bassinette. The King's seizures came and went unpredictably. Bessa tripped over the lawn in the early morning, at the hour when the chicory was all flagrant. All this garbage had piled up on him in the last few days. He had been abandoned and she had abandoned him. Perhaps I can illustrate this point. By 1613, he had abandoned verse altogether. Grandmother's acknowledged prejudice was a family matter. I turn to the operational record. The fact of social pressure is undeniable. Towards noon, whales were raised. Whales in the interior? Whales in the sea, seen and catalogued by men from the interior riding ships. The seizures of the King became frightening to those forced to watch them, he gnawed at himself, he recognized no one. Messages were delivered by scowling boys in livery about the sighting of whales. The King's seizures became, themselves, imperious. I put to you the facts. When it has the opportunity to do so, a lion will eat a truly huge meal. The King hurled himself upon the ladies in waiting to the Queen, if you could call them that, for in truth they were pokojówkas, and had to be restrained, soothed, by gentle words and rose water on velvet, and yellow petits four. "I will meet up with her in the hut by the river," he murmured over and over. Passegrain the jester flapped his stick, sat moping in the corner. "In the corner, in the shadow, in the darkness. Not to move, not to see, not to know." The jester was on his head now, and the pokojówkas were rushing in and out of the place with ceremonial platters of pomegranate seeds and little honey cakes.

BENGAL

has always been India's most populous province. Carriages wound in spirals around the great fountain. The Maharajah of Nayadwip has long been India's most prosperous ruler. They could hardly bear to part with us when at last the story came to an end. The Rajah of Bhagalpur has seventeen thousand head of elephant. The idea of an art without visual appeal was discussed. Grapes were stored. The King was revived and put on a litter. They put in with bankers for shares. Stratos and Lammorghini caused huge boulders to be moved from the island to the mainland, and then changed their minds. The idea of an art without visual appeal was put forward. Vermilion satin was bought by the bolt. "You're a credit to your country, sir, that's what you are," said Passegrain to the King, who glared at him in silence. Glared in silence, stared in silence, compared in silence. Grantley came from the Queen of England as a Special Emissary, brought the skin of a tiger, asked if they had a portrait of the lost Prince Regent, Charles Maximilian. "We do not keep portraits," they replied, perhaps a little too sententiously, because there was provocation. Vast polemics limned the corridor, emblazoned on bronzed shields and faded blue banners of silk. He went looking through the vast assortment of chambers. "Ha, ha!" cackled the yellow old czarownica. Some plots are simple while others are complex. A blinding light shone through the curtains. The lovers stood in the deserted room, fondling one another with phrases. The lovers stood gazing at what was given to the gaze. The lovers stood. A blinding light shone. The yellow, beaten, cynical old czarownica ate a root, chewed a piece of fat, drank wine, cursed the lovers who stood in the deserted room, the lovers who saw, the lovers near the stained glass, the two lovers. The old czarownica revived the King. Grapes were pressed. The lovers stood.

A LION WILL EAT

a truly large meal when it has the opportunity to do so. Perhaps I can illustrate this point. I put to you the facts. As I continue to build up data, the perspective becomes cloudy, but I shall not cede my purpose: to put the facts to you, illustrating this point. Perhaps Bessa came down for the weekend. Green beans had to be tipped in quantity. The tipping of the green beans—truly they were more blue than green—in the old kitchen by the hazy windowlight, at the old hands of the czarownica. The King's seizures came and went unpredictably. Cats in general, big ones and small, desire contact more than imagery, and are consequently betrayed by illumination; humans can learn to prefer light, however, to touch. Perhaps I can illustrate this point.

HE WAS HELPLESS,

but worse than helpless he was miserable. He
had experienced the hunger. Grantley came from
the Queen of England and beseeched a portrait,
"Might I see a portrait? The lost Prince Regent.
Maximilian Charles." The animal was acquitted
on the ground that she was the victim of violence.
"Ha, ha!" cackled the old witch-lady, "I curse you!"
Grandmother's acknowledged prejudice was a
family matter. I am speaking at present solely of
our own childhood. The man who wrote the note
is a German, probably from Schleswig-Holstein.
I'll never be able to manage. Truly the usefulness
of a calling, therefore its favor in the sight of God,
is esteemed first in moral terms, in terms of the value of the goods produced in it for the community.
Bessa tripped over the lawn in the early morning.
What a beauty! She danced first with a tall man
covered with hay. There are only two more things
that need to be said here. Towards noon whales
were raised. The idea of an art without visual appeal was put forward.

JOHANNES BEGG

was probably born in Austria in 1690 without thighs or legs. He was helpless, but worse than helpless he was miserable, his greatest misery being an overwhelming sense that his compatriots considered him to be brave. The fact of social pressure is undeniable. You can struggle to escape, so routinely that you feel nothing, but escape is inconceivable, or so it says in the treatise. The man who wrote the treatise was a German, probably from Schleswig-Holstein. Antonio asked if they had portraits of Charles Maximilian, and of Maximilian Charles, and of Maximilian. Carriages wound in spirals round the great fountain. Some plots are simple while others are complex. I turn to the operational record. I am speaking at present solely of our childhood. A lion will eat a truly large meal when it has the opportunity to do so. Bengal has always been India's most populous province. The Raman of Nayabandara kept mice. This thought had already been expressed. For a jolt to the system, try reading this aloud. Flowers poured out of alabaster and were a stream upon their shoulders.

The King's seizures came and went. Some plots are simple while others are complex. The King's seizures came and went. The King had, and then didn't have, seizures.

ASTERS POURED

out of alabaster. Why were all flowers so beautiful and yet so hapless? I am speaking at present solely of our own childhood. "In all things it is the beginnings and ends that are interesting," Berridge said, quoting Kenko. Or paraphrasing Kenko. Or quoting Kenko Masa-san. A blinding light shone through the curtains. At five, the Marquis made an exit. When Mathilda came down in her silver slippers and her silver tights, Berridge rose to admire her. What a beauty! By 1613, he had abandoned verse altogether. The Marquis had never been informed of the limitations that obtained for persons in his circumstance, and now that the rainy season had come and the townspeople were settled into their retreats, he ventured to explore, insofar as resource would permit, the extent of his territories. The King's seizures came and went unpredictably.

WAYLAID IN THE VAST AUTUMNAL FOREST,

the courier arrived too late. When finally he jumped down from his sweating horse and ran up to them, they cried, "Too late! It is done!" The courier fell to the ground, his chest heaving. The carriages raced and rattled upon the carpet of leaves, under the chartreuse trees which receded in the chartreuse light, and the courier was outrun, halted, made to dismount, lashed to a tree trunk, blindfolded, branded upon his shoulder. He lay exhausted for an incalculable time. He remounted and rode on, the bravest of men, but arrived late. "Too late!" Flowers poured out of alabaster. The man who wrote the treatise was a German, not from Schleswig-Holstein, from the Schwarzenwald. The fact of social pressure is undeniable. He had been abandoned and she had abandoned him. Two carriages were racing, and a woman in the second one wore dark green velvet and the carriages rattled the leaves. Bengal has always been India's most populous province. The King's seizures came and went unpredictably. In the garden, mosquitoes replicated. She realized with a start that she had been presenting herself to him as a co-nundrum. The King was reprieved. Grandmother's acknowledged prejudice was a family matter. Flowers poured out of alabaster and were a stream upon their shoulders. The idea of an art without visual appeal was put forward. Cats in general, big ones and small, desire contact more than imagery, and are consequently betrayed by illumination. The château was empty and shortly after arriving there the carriages swept around and drew away in haste. A breeze tickled the hazelnut trees that clus-tered at the margins of the great forest. A woman in the second carriage wore dark green velvet and the carriages rattled the leaves. The seizures of the King were both painful and hallucinatory, both torporous and constipating, both debilitating and riddling. The King imagined the naked lovers. The King's seizures came and went unpredictably. The lovers stood in the deserted room, a dank room, its walls laid with tapestries. Their bodies glisten-ing. . . . The fact of social pressure is undeniable. The château was empty. No one could identify the lovers. The King's seizures came and went. The lov-ers stood in the deserted room. The King was alive to the moment. The lovers locked in a permanent embrace in the corner, under the De Heem, in shadow, in darkness. Grandmother's lips remained open. Seventeen thousand elephants. The carriages swept around and drew away in haste.

Dream Escapes

THEY WERE ALL CHILDREN OF THEIR TIME.

Chamberlain had always been happy to rent his shelter. From it came several drawings and paintings. It was a riveting sight. She was filled with guilt and a sense of failing which made her drowsy. A cozy fire burns in the hearth. Certainly it is the movement of color within—particularly the blue and the yellow—that affords the château its warmth. You should really have seen the transformation. It was very cold on the morning of my last visit; I was not yet well; the château was nearly empty. He adored literature. If you have difficulty keeping your eyes off the hostess's collection of Nabi paintings, it is understandable.

A cozy fire burns in the hearth.

Ample, pastel slipcovers. For precisely an hour, or perhaps a little less, it was very cold on the morning of my last visit; I was not yet well; the château was nearly empty. I was not yet well, I languished. I swam in the long river of fever.

TEA AND TOAST.

Tea and toast.
The jumping horse
Is loved the most.
Tea and toast.
Toast and tea.
Will she who loves
the horse love me?

CLAMSHELLS

smell like—well, old clams. Chartreuse silks and white gloves were nothing but mass production in any part of my life. Change is what we cannot escape. My statement had already been expressed. Many speak of it that way. I have always enjoyed bits and pieces, an existence devoted to "tiny breaths and intimations of beauty." Change is what we cannot escape. "I grew up surrounded by shells and coral," she says. Change is what we cannot escape. Think of it as a vagary of the creative life. "If you're from Russia," he says, "You cannot escape. You cannot escape an existence devoted to 'tiny breaths and intimations of beauty.'" Speak of it. His second son, Jonville, inherited, placed under management, and then did everything within his power to distance himself from, the place. Will she who loved the horse love me? Tea and toast, toast and tea.

THE BLACK STONES

are limestone from Liguria, the white ones are quartz from Ticino. Quartz from Ticino, white as night.

DEFICIENT RESEARCH

led quickly to a major historical error. My statement had already been expressed. For precisely an hour, or perhaps a little less, a lugubrious gentleman in chartreuse silks and white gloves will pass champagne. It was very cold on the morning of my last visit; I was not yet well; the château was nearly empty. They had moved out the furniture and the window dressings. The château was all but empty—I know, I was there. Who else serves bite-sized club sandwiches at tea? For precisely an hour, or perhaps a little less, a lugubrious gentleman in a chartreuse silk waistcoat and white gloves will pass champagne. Champagne and toast, champagne and tea. Chamberlain had always been happy to rent his shelter. It was very cold on the morning of my last visit; I was not yet well; the château was nearly empty. I was there, you could have found me if you had made the effort. For precisely an hour, or perhaps a little less, a lugubrious gentleman will pass champagne. Chartreuse silks. White gloves. A cozy fire burns in the hearth.

A COZY FIRE

burns in the hearth. Surprisingly perhaps, there is
no art to be seen here or in any other room. My
statement had already been expressed. For almost
ninety years in this compound, an ever-broadening
stream of gifted poets, composers, painters, writers, filmmakers, and photographers has triumphed
in escaping the conventional discomfitures of the
workaday world in order to pass a few months of
intense, self-delighting labor in the evergreen fastness of our studios guarded all day from interruptions. "I love," said he, "to quote. I adore literature.
Literary traditions became a part of me. I was a
child of my time." He said, "I played as a boy with
garter snakes and voles. I invented communities."
He adored literature, and literary traditions became a part of him. His second son, Jonville, inherited, placed under management, and then did
everything within his power to distance himself
from, the place. They were all children of their
time. "I grew up surrounded," said she, "by shells
and coral. Shells were around my head, shells were
under my feet. Coral was upon my walls, chipped,

pasted. Coral was upon my walls. I grew up among coral and shells. I was a fish. My childhood was a lagoon." Toast and tea. Much depends on illusion. The black stones are limestone from Liguria, the white ones are quartz from Ticino.

THE MISTRESS REQUIRES
DARKNESS BLACK AS PITCH

in order to sleep. "I grew up surrounded by shells and coral, coral and shells," she says. Much depends on illusion. I have always enjoyed bits and pieces. "If you're from Russia," he says, and there is nothing pleasant in his voice, "You understand mass production genetically. I spent twenty-eight years there and I feel there was nothing but mass production in any part of my life." Much depends on illusion. "I spent twenty-eight years there," he says. I have always enjoyed bits and pieces. Much depends on bits and pieces. I have always enjoyed illusion. Much depends on decoupage, much depends on a menagerie, much depends on cuisine, much depends on whether from the vault of earth we can exploit the geological capital instead of the agricultural interest—this from Billington. And so much depends upon smelting. I have always required darkness black as pitch in order to sleep. Modern man works even in his dreams. "What most people don't want, I love," he says. There is in his voice nothing pleasant. A fire is in the hearth, a cozy fire. The birds are overhead, screaming. The importunate birds. A gentleman in lugubrious silks with a chartreuse waistcoat pours champagne, a child of his time. They were all children. "If you're from Russia," he says, "you understand mass production genetically." Much depends on illusion. "If you're from Russia," he says, "you understand mass production. What most people don't want, I love." They did sit in a circle in the great station on Rood Street, announcing to one another where they were from, tracing their roots, but no one knew where he was going. Porters lit gas lamps and an odd white luminescence filled the foggy place, reflecting the moisture and drawing up to the surface of the eye all types of verdigris and moss, of pitted bronze plaquery, the hollow eyes of children, rice, chameleons. Clamshells smell like—well, old clams.

FOR OCCASIONAL FORMAL NIGHTTIME GATHERINGS,

the dry, ample pastel slipcovers were stored, revealing jewel-toned upholstery with a perfectly tailored, Eglantine look. Jewel-toned upholstery. Jeweled and toned upholstery. Jeweled, toned, and jewel-toned. Upholstery as green as emeralds, as pink as opals, lost in the night, the need to be journeying, the feet of the chairs carved into paws and embraced by children needing an anchor in the moving jeweled sea of sensation. Hard candies. Jewels on wrists laid upon the arms of the jewel-toned upholstery. Tonics in the tea. A large swollen beaker of emerald tonic, a crystal amphora. An Eglantine look. A tailored, Eglantine look. Ample, pastel slipcovers. Occasional formal nighttime gatherings. Once or twice a fortnight. White tie, tails, top hat; top hat, white tie, and tails. Lost in the night. The carriage swooping into the unlit park, the stars, the chill in the air, his ivory-tipped walking stick, the scent of jasmine on her neck, duck swimming darkly in darkness on the Serpentine, sleepless dreams, the smell of roasting chestnuts at Marble Arch, reclusiveness, tall elms, unfurnished flats after the war, spats, pittely-pattely-pat, the prowling cat, the glistening cravat, the willingness of the sun to set. For occasional formal nighttime gatherings the mistress required darkness in order to sleep. The mistress made her requirements known, but said nothing. Sounds came through the fireplace. Think of it as a vagary of the creative life; many speak of it that way; in an existence devoted to "tiny breaths and intimations of beauty," the only constant is change. Change is what we cannot escape. Chamberlain loved to rent his place. There was toast and there was tea, and little cakes, and savories for the toast. There was a little china jar of anchovy paste from Fortnum's. For precisely an hour, or perhaps a little less, a lugubrious gentleman in chartreuse silks and white gloves passed champagne. Chamberlain drove off for occasional formal nighttime gatherings. The only constant is change. He was told to park off-lot.

ON-LOT PARKING IS BETTER
THAN OFF-LOT PARKING.

On-lot parking is in the swimming pool. Off-lot parking closes at sundown. On-lot parking is adjacent the gardenia hedges. Surprisingly perhaps, he was told to park off-lot. He parked off-lot. He wished he could have parked on-lot. On-lot parking is better. They have tall hedges of flowering gardenia, bordering the on-lot parking, hedges twenty feet tall, taller than elephants, the perfume suffocating, but you need a blue ticket, and he was given only an orange ticket. The swimming pool is being used, has been filled, there are little ships, Roman galleys. The gardenia hedges cannot be seen in the darkness that the mistress requires in order to sleep. He parked. He drove on-lot, then drove off-lot, and parked off-lot, and walked back on-lot, and the gardenia hedges brushed him, and they speedily got to work painting his face.

SURPRISING PERHAPS, THERE IS NO ART TO BE SEEN HERE OR IN ANY OTHER ROOM.

A riveting sight. She was filled with guilt and a sense of failing which made her drowsy. My statement had already been expressed, I felt, and yet there was some delicious mortifying sense of not having been heard. Seated upon a bench just within the Bellerive garden wall, one stares past mixed borders of artichokes and hazelnut trees and dense nasturtiums to a high circular holly hedge. Chamberlain had always been happy to rent his shelter. Deficient research. Distance. Bits and pieces. Who else serves? You can search the by-ways. Chamberlain had always been happy. It was very cold on the morning of my last visit; I was not yet well; the château was nearly empty. A cozy fire burns in the hearth. For almost ninety years, an ever-broadening stream of gifted poets, composers, ceramicists, singers, and discus throwers has triumphed in escaping the workaday world in order to pass a few days of self-flagellating labor in the secret green fastness of our studios guarded all day from interruptions. Park off-lot. Snails. Artichokes and hazelnut trees. A bench. Mixed borders. Dense nasturtiums. A hedge. A high circular hedge, holly, the Holly Hedge. A gardenia hedge, dense, perfumed, taller than elephants. Dense mixed borders. Dense hazelnut trees. A little stone wall with a moving snail, a fat snail, at the turn of evening, with the smell of clams. Surprisingly perhaps, there is no art to be seen here or in any other room. He adored literature, and literary traditions became a part of him. Who else serves bite-sized club sandwiches at tea? "What most people don't want," he says, "I love." Park off-lot. Park off-lot. No, sorry, park off-lot. Could you please park off-lot. Park off-lot, please. Sorry, please, no, park off-lot. On the other hand, park on-lot. No, yes, park on-lot, over there. No, sorry, off-lot. No, off-lot. Leave your vehicle under the holly hedge there and come here and call. Call 6-2-6-1 and ask for your party. Leave your car there and come here. Come here. Call from here. Call the number you have been given, or call 6-2-6-1 and ask for your party, and see if they have authorization for you. Much depends on illusion.

MUCH DEPENDS ON ILLUSION.

They wanted Stage 12 but they couldn't use it because the château wasn't finished, it was empty, and
the heat was down. The heat was completely down.
The mistress requires darkness black as pitch in
order to sleep. Curtains are pulled, three layers.
A story is told of an old gamekeeper who walked
through his forest and found a cave, and entered
the cave and found a package tied with string, who
opened the package with his knife and found a
box, who opened the box and found a jeweled frog
with a hinged back, all pure silver, who opened
the frog and found a piece of paper tightly folded.
They used Stage 18, the one with the false floor. Yellow paper, folded and creased with a creasing iron.
Climb the staircase to the floor above. Climb the
staircase to the floor above that. Keep climbing.
"What most people don't want, I love," he says.
The mistress sleeps, and next to her bedroom is a
gardenia hedge, tall as elephants. There is a swimming pool, the size of a mogul's cottage. She sleeps
and no one touches her. Much depends on illusion.
Hair comes in, fixes a curl. Climb the staircase, she

sleeps. They were all children of their time. Climb, much depends on illusion, there are savories and also sweets, there are jams, there are tiny plates of smoked fish and also tiny smoked fishes. The mistress requires pitch darkness in order to sleep. A candle in the corridor will awake her. You suddenly find yourself in another régime, walking the corridors of a gilded palace. Deficient research led quickly to a major historical error, that the writers couldn't fix: there reigned not one but two royal families. Much depends on the illusion of one suddenly finding oneself. In order to sleep, change is what we cannot escape. We have always enjoyed his second son, Jonville. If one has difficulty keeping one's eyes off the hostess's collection of Nabi paintings, it is understandable. If you have difficulty, see the mistress. The mistress is not the hostess, and this is the cause of the confusion, so that the many corridors take on an equivalency and the tapestries do not guide us. But there are two royal families. One must consult the mistress about the hostess. She will see you but she cannot see you now for at least an hour. For precisely an hour, or perhaps a little less, he adored literature. Clamshells smell like—well, bite-sized club sandwiches at tea. It was difficult to read altogether because of the pervasive stench of the clams. Then they came with their money. You could buy snow and have it delivered. You could buy anything. You should really have seen the transformation. Certainly it is the movement of color within that is most impressive. They were all children of their time. The furniture was all of a piece, with the feet carved into paws. Neither the mistress nor the hostess leaves the property, you'll never come across them at the local cheese shop. "I grew up surrounded by shells and coral," she says. Much depends on illusion. As well, the mistress requires pitch darkness in order to sleep. As well, the mistress requires darkness black as pitch in order to sleep. The hostess proclaims, "I grew up surrounded." The color seems to move up the walls, to climb the stairs to the next level, to infuse itself into the old portraits of men long dead now calculating from the walls. "What most people don't want, I love." Think of it as a vagary of the creative life; many speak of it that way. Many speak of it. Many speak of it as a vagary. Stage 18. Many intimations, many vagaries, many quiet comments. There is heat on Stage 18, everything is ready. Many speak.

CLAMSHELLS SMELL LIKE—
WELL, OLD CLAMS.

Clamshells smell like—well, unwashed beakers.
No. Clamshells smell like—well, stored slipcovers.
No. Clamshells smell like—well, a cold château.
No. Clamshells smell like—well, bite-sized club
sandwiches? Champagne? Upholstery? Clam-
shells smell like—well, a major historical error.

THEY WERE ALL CHILDREN OF THEIR TIME.

They were all children. Think of it as a vagary of the creative life. I grew up. Pastel slipcovers were stored, revealing jewel-toned upholstery. On the morning of my last visit, I was not yet well. On the morning of his last visit literary traditions became a part of him. The only constant is change. Change is what we cannot escape.

> Toast and tea.
> Toast and tea.
> Under the spreading
> Lilac tree.

Very cold. Just within the Bellerive garden wall, one stares. There is no art to be seen. Pass a few months here in our studios. A sense of failing made her drowsy. My statement had already been expressed. You should really have *seen*. Here or in any other room. Bits and pieces. What we cannot escape: a perfectly tailored, Eglantine look. Well, old clams.

THE BLACK STONES

are limestone from Liguria, the white ones are quartz from Ticino. The black stones are limestone from Liguria, the white ones are quartz from Ticino. The black stones are limestone from Liguria, the white ones are quartz from Ticino. The black stones are limestone from Liguria, the white ones are quartz from Ticino. The black stones are limestone from Liguria, the white ones are quartz from Ticino. I have always enjoyed bits and pieces. The mistress requires black darkness in order to sleep.

HE PARKED OFF-LOT.

A darkness black as pitch permitted him to sleep.
Liguria was sunny, with black stones everywhere.
Historical errors were committed there, and here;
here and there. The château, happily, was finished.
Jonville tore down the château later. The traffic police waited at the exit and trapped people coming
into town, pecking away at their pads like so many
woodpeckers, nibbling sandwiches from tea-trol-
lies eccentric in this part of the lot. The mistress
required darkness black as pitch, but since he had
had it, she could not have it. They were children
of their time. The mistress parked on-lot. Jonville
made sandwiches for tea. He commanded the de-
livery of a little tea trolley and they built it and he
loaded it and wheeled it and then, when it was all
over, set it aflame. The break-up of our camp, as it
were. Gentlemen in mauve changed into turquoise
and served tea and made sandwiches and parked
off-lot and made historical errors and rented the
château and razed the château and adored literary
traditions but stood at fountains counting pea-
cocks, children of their time, nibbling, sleeping in

darkness, history rebounding into itself, the gardenias in bloom, suffocating perfume, the snow that you could buy delivered, laid out, darkness settling in, the pool drained, three curtains drawn, the upholstery revealed, climbing to the floor above. Much depended upon illusion. Historical errors committed. Park off-lot. Climb the stairs.

Introduction

Introduction

1.

We dream in chains. Dreams come swiftly upon one another, some short-lived as breaths and others spun out into tissues, almost organs. We do not understand the extent, the depth, the attenuation, the plasticity, the hesitancy, the coloration, the persistence of our dreams.

2.

We are both inside and outside our dreams, and our dreams conflate (and confabulate) the inside and the outside as a single space. We move in our dreams, the dreams move around us, and we are static in our dreams as we move. We move without accomplishing. We move without tracing our steps, so that it is nothing in our dreams to recapitulate the same territory. Paul Newman said that when (in 1986) he was working with Martin Scorsese, they were shooting a scene in a bar. After each take Scorsese got up and walked around and around and around like a chickling hunting for feed. It is nothing in our dreams to recapitulate the same territory; as every recapitulation is a new passage, there are no recapitulations. But it is also nothing to have the feeling of having been here *before*: the *déjà vu*, because everything in dream is seen before, is *vu déjà*, and also everything has never been seen. Because everything has never been seen we gaze at it enraptured and move through it in awe. But everything has been seen. I stood once in Colorado in high red rocks, the Garden of the Gods, and the sky was blue, and the air was sweet, and I had a red sweater, I am telling you.

3.

We cannot tell pleasant dreams from *cauchemars* until we are no longer dreaming. They are all similarly unintelligible, but when we awaken and look back, and if we can remember, we describe our dreams and catalogue them, remember their contents and qualities. How, looking back, do we know good from bad? By hoping and not hoping. I have files and files with shrapnel of thought, torn pieces of paper, napkins, matchbook covers—"They're onto you. I'm in your bedroom."—index cards, green index cards, pink index cards, yellow index cards, blue index cards, white index cards, on which

I have written lines, quotations, more lines, rhymes, questions, words, names, the names of movies, the names of foods and places, the addresses I have found in my relentless search, my search for I know not what, in cities, in towns, cities at night, cities at night in the rain, addresses on rainy streets in the cities, flowers, mustards, rocks, smashed rocks. "Stop Freuding me!" says Hitchcock's Marnie to Mark, inventing a verb. *Ich freude, du freudst, er freudt, wir freuden*. Great fat lips embracing my face. The beach empty, stoneless. Great fat lips kissing my face, my eyes. Fat wet lips kissing my eyes. The deep files are buried underneath a mountain in the central United States, in Kansas—are there mountains in Kansas? The deep files are buried in Kansas. You need a green pass, it's virtually impossible to get one. You go a couple of thousand feet below ground in a series of elevators, until you feel like a carton of eggs that has been squashed by an elephant. That is where the deep files are. How are they arranged? It is a salt mine, to keep the air sterile. They are arranged, of course, by number. How are the numbers arranged? You go to Kansas. Great fat lips kissed my face but I kiss your face in tenderness. I keep everything. Every shred of paper with every number, every word, and afterward I know what is pleasant and what is a taste of hell, if I know hell, if I know anything. A man named Annabel came to do cabinetry and soaped his screws. "Yes, that's right," he said, "Yes, that's right. *Oui, c'est comme ça.* On each screw, a little soap." Often I think I am in the middle of a pleasant dream and later, only later, I learn it was a nightmare.

4.

Our dreams cannot, in a way, belong to us. The light dipping into the autumn garden was chartreuse. Great fat lips embraced my face. The beach, empty, stoneless. Great fat lips kissed my face, my eyes. Fat wet lips kissed my eyes. I am dreaming my aunt when I was a little boy, aged six, and I had never seen her before, and she came to me crying. She was enormous and dignified, and her mouth had intent. Her eyes like knives. But I am also dreaming a character of Fellini's, from *Amarcord*, who was therefore a part of his dream and has become a part of mine. The characters of my dream are taken from his dream, and his dream characters come from another dream. Catfish are jumpin' and the cotton is high. A man named Annabel came to do cabinetry and soaped his screws. He had blue eyes and a serious mouth and his work with wood was exceptional and swift. Now and forever.

5.

Let me tell you about the movies. I went as a child into the great dark spaces, the sweet-smelling red velvet spaces, with the high golden cupolas and the gaping wall in which the world came alive. I thought at first that giants were playing behind some great taut sheet. Then I learned it was something else, but a something that was not identified. Over and over, I went to see this great essence, studying, as though they were glyphs in Talmud, those faces on the voyage to *Botany Bay*—Alan Ladd, Cedric Hardwicke, and the terrifying silences of James Mason—and the islanders of Fiji in *His Majesty O'Keefe*—particularly Abraham Sofaer as Fatumak—and Dorothy Lamour, scarlet by moonlight, somehow intoxicatingly twisting, in *The Road to Bali*, invoking a space that should not have been familiar but was familiar and from a time I could not position, a moonlight time, all long gone, and Jimmy Stewart and Cornel Wilde and Betty Hutton in *The Greatest Show on Earth*, Johnny Weissmuller in *Tarzan the Ape Man*, all of this again and again, *The Incredible Shrinking*

Man, and Christopher Olsen and Reginald Nalder and Brenda de Banzie in *The Man Who Knew Too Much*, again and again and again, whatever will be, will be. Every nuance I froze and examined, every line, every shape. The colors were disarming and intoxicating, were motors that hurled me out of the gravitational pull of daily thought. There was a pineapple green in *The Greatest Show on Earth*. In *Boy on a Dolphin*, there was a chopping royal blue sea. In *His Majesty O'Keefe*, the water had a little green in it, and whitecaps, the hot breath of the sun. There was a daffodil yellow dress worn by Susan Hayward one afternoon—one afternoon for me, but also eternity—as she sang (clap-clap-clap-clap) "Deep in the Heart of Texas." There were fawn green branches around Doris Day singing "Secret Love" in *Calamity Jane*. The soft furniture in Dean Jagger's woody lodge in *White Christmas*. *There's No Business Like Show Business* had everything, and Donald O'Connor dancing around sculptures moving in strange purple water, and Marilyn Monroe, who was boring to listen to but who was at the same time aflame. One couldn't touch all this, yet one's eyes swallowed, and one couldn't digest it, so that it resided within oneself undigested and revolving, irritating and pleasantly raw, until finally it was crystallized. Later on, one learned that motion pictures were made by people, and who made them, one listed the names, one had seen *The Bridges at Toko-Ri* and came to know that Henry Bumstead designed it, and one sought to touch the world of these makers of images even as one had sought to touch the images. Where to find them? They were in the files. They were in the files in deep storage, under that mountain, in Kansas, under a mountain in Tennessee, under a mountain in Colorado, three thousand feet down, catalogued by number, under a street in Beverly Hills, catalogued in boxes, written in pencil, typed on onionskin, pink onionskin, white onionskin, yellow onionskin, inscribed on daily report forms, scribbled on letterhead, the mythic names on the mythic letterhead, the names of those who have vanished, VERBAL MESSAGES CAUSE MIS-UNDERSTANDING AND DELAYS PLEASE PUT THEM IN WRITING, Barney Balaban, Jacob H. Karp, William Meiklejohn, Luigi Luraschi, Roy Fjastad, Farciot Edouart, Richard Mealand, Edouard de Segonzac, "Jerry" Juran, A. Arnold Gillespie, . . . I went to the files, I couldn't touch, I ate through my eyes, I envisioned coffee tables, I envisioned a sofa with a coffee table with a paint-

ing on the wall and a plate glass window looking
out upon cypress trees, I envisioned black coffee,
I envisioned an apron, aqua blue, a hairdo, finger-
nail polish, wall-to-wall broadloom, my father, my
father's hand, my father driving the car in winter,
aqua blue, my father laughing, my father laughing
with my mother, my mother's hair, my mother's asparagus and cheese roll-ups, my father drank rye,
now and forever, now and forever, Jimmy Stewart
reached out, Doris Day was afraid, there is a story
about how Doris Day was afraid when for Hitchcock she was acting afraid, and Hitchcock never
said much, and this made it worse, and Jimmy told
her, "Don't worry," and Hitchcock never took his
tie off, even in a hundred-and-thirty degree heat
in Marrakech, where there was a revolution in
progress, where the Glaoui had to be kept happy,
all this in crystals now. Is it a sick love if it has utterly crystallized, if one has devoured through the
eyes? Colors marched upon me before I knew. My
father and mother went to Mexico and came back
with magical maracas, varnished, deeply colored,
and these became holy objects, plum red, and with
pictures of the Aztec mosaics at the University,
the flowers draped over the canals. Tarzan went
to the elephants' graveyard, a chalky and horrible

place, more horrible, no doubt, because it was in black and white, and the white men stood watching with trembling jaws. It was and is an unending voyage, and spectacle is nothing but the method of bringing it in. In, always in, to the deepest chambers, which hold, perhaps, not buried memories but unfulfilled hopes. Gene Tierney in *The Egyptian*, the soft white teeth, and then in *Leave Her to Heaven*—"then": history is a chain of experiences—riding a chestnut brown horse at sunset in the hills of Taos, scattering her father's ashes to the beat of a drum, Guy Madison in *Attack at Feather River*, the beat of the drum, the maracas, the train going off the tracks in *The Greatest Show on Earth*, again and again and again and again, the blue lights at midnight, emergency lights, ambulances, the bodies, the blue lights, the running, the escaping lions, the cries, the pineapple green under the big top, the elephants on parade, the sound of a triangle and a xylophone, girls in purple plumes, sawdust. The dust in libraries may settle on critical treatises about suture, about the filmic signifier, about the empowering gaze, about labor and capital in early Hollywood, but now and forever what is crystallized inside me is only the big top, the Indians attacking at Feather River, "Deep in the Heart of

Texas," the rocky pathways of the old west, the way that Dan Dailey, dancing, used his hands. I saw in a dream Dan Dailey using his hands, throwing them out away from his center of balance, his face looking in the opposite direction, and he was on his way to a promised land, he was on his way. O Lord, he was on his way.

6.

Some dreams move slowly and some dreams move quickly but all dreams move at the same speed.

7.

I fell once from a balcony of a yellow brick building, once, decades and decades ago, and the other night in a dream I was back there, and the building still stood, with all the buildings that had been around it gone, reduced, leveled to bricks on the ground, yet this building was faded and present, present and faded, and I looked up and saw the window of a tiny bathroom in which accidentally I had locked myself, the window through which firemen came on their ladder and in their thick tan coats to help me be free. There was no balcony, but I fell from the balcony, again and again and again, backwards. I fell backwards, never hitting the ground. My father stood watching, aghast. As the ground approached I was yanked upward, as though on a bungee cord, but this was years before I knew of the bungee cord, which had existed already, it seems, for ten or twelve years. I had this dream for years, over and over, at least once a month. Someone said to me, when I was ten or eleven years old, that if one ever dreams of falling and actually hits the ground in the dream, that is death. I have another recurring dream, of traveling with her to Nice—in my dream the place is called Nice. I have been many times to Nice in my waking life and it does not correspond to the Nice of my dream. (Which is the real Nice?) I go with her to Nice and we cross from one island over to a second island (the real Nice has no islands), worried always about catching our flight back in time, because it is an important flight in a huge jet where we will sit near the rear with potted ferns, and sometimes we land in a place that is identified as New Zealand and that is south of Australia, an island, and that has white beaches; but now instead we cross over a narrow turquoise channel that turns ultramarine just as we are crossing it, in a barge of sorts, and we come to a rocky place where if you go on the right road you come to a wonderful restaurant. And there they serve something wonderful in a fabulous sauce, but I cannot say what it is. I know for a fact that I am entranced by the *quenelles de brochet Nantua* you can have in Nice, or that you could have had once, at a jangling and fabulous place that has vanished—there were colored lights, it was called the Grand Café de Lyon and now it is in my dreams—but in this dream restaurant it is not *quenelles*, but the taste is exciting in the same way. And the landlady is waiting for us with our room, in which there is a fern, and she is old and wears lace and is anxious. Too anxious. And we are very late, we have not kept our engagement. But we owe her rent and she is upset, but she is polite. She does her hair. And there is another dream, inspired by childhood journeys with my parents, where I am borne in a speeding automobile on a new highway toward a tall, tall, tall, architecturally fabulous bridge that spans a horrible chasm—into which I am afraid that I will fall—and we are going up on the bridge, up, up, up into the sky, all I can see is the sky, a too narrow, too tall bridge too far over the too black chasm, and we come to a city, or part of a city, and there are little buildings which are crammed near one another in a shabby district to my left, a district where the buildings are yellow, and it is vital, more than vital, that I find the correct building, and for the return voyage I have to navigate that bridge in that automobile, alone. And there is a version of this dream where the return voyage is modified: after crossing the bridge I am somehow flying an airplane, my vehicle actually becomes an airplane and takes off, and it is luxurious with the cold air smacking me right in the face, and where I land it is called Cleveland, but it is not Cleveland, and there is a huge tarmac and I am standing on it, there are palm trees, luscious, I am late for a flight to somewhere else. We are both late for a flight. We are rushing, we will be the last ones on. The stewardess is wearing powder blue, smiling, gracious. The plane has ferns in the back, my seat is elevated, very sumptuously upholstered. We are flying to the bottom of the world, tropical islands. Great yellow striding birds. Back on the tarmac. Palm trees all round. Late. The round terminal, the terminal shaped like a lima bean and also a knife, from counter to counter, to check in bags, to get red and white tickets, past hordes of people, directed here, there, the ticket counters piled level on level. Running through the airport with her, from counter to counter, looking for the ticket counter, but we are going to miss the flight. Or is it a train? I am running on the tarmac, across painted white lines, and the planes are taxiing out to the runways. Even now the flight is going, and there are trains, trains are going, we hop onto a train, the train is like a plane inside, we are seated near the front but we must get off on a platform and go to the rear. We go into the plane from the rear door, where there is a uniformed stewardess being very businesslike and polite, and it is sunset. And the air on the tarmac is cool and tropical. There are palm trees. I awake too soon, before the understanding. Pieces break away and become mist.

8.

Words cease to hold their own magic when they are taken out of their beds. When they sit in my hand, away from their beds in contexts, words take on my own magic. I hold them and they assume colorations that are distinct and impossible to speak about. I can say "forest green," but there is a way the sunlight shines through this—for example, among the glistening redwoods of Lighthouse Park in North Vancouver—that I cannot describe. Wylie Sypher writes of the gothic light *through* as contrasted against the impressionistic light *upon*. I am looking at pages of an ancient encyclopedia with colored reproductions of jewel stones. Words have sounds and colors. Or let me say, words have colors and colors have sounds. Colors have sounds, exactly as (Skriabine knew this) sounds have colors. So, words ring. When in my dreams I am speaking, the voice does not come out of my mouth or my head, it comes out of my chest, and I am powerless either to curtail it or to shape what it says, but I am obliged to listen to it carefully. Words have nothing intrinsically to do with action but can be added to action. Intrinsically (Goodman knew this) action is silent. Another way: words themselves are actions, not references to action. The boy walks down the street to buy raisins at the corner store. This is not me, though I did walk down the street to buy raisins for my grandmother, so she could put them in her buns. I can smell the yeasty sweetness of the buns, rising, glazed, filling all the kitchen (all white-painted) with that sweetness. The boy walks down the street. Somebody is watching him. My grandmother had boxes of grapes ready for making wine, and all the air was a perfume of them, and of the hewn firewood in stacks. Trains backed up behind her house, smelling of oil and steel and the cold. I am not saying that all this happened, but it is happening in my saying it.

9.

Somebody is watching the boy walking down the street, wearing shorts, in the cold, the bitter cold, toward the corner. He has been in the sweet-smelling store, has collected raisins in a little brown paper bag, is walking back down the street, and somebody on the other side of the road is watching him. Of course he knows who it is but he also does not know who it is and somebody is watching and he does not know that he knows who it is, the person watching, and does not know that he knows that he walks. Somebody is watching, standing in front of a pale green house, noting everything, and will write a book. The boy will be written into a book and will become a dream.

10.

Boy marches down street. We sense the echo but we do not comprehend its meaning. Boy walks. The boy walks down the street to buy—let it be raisins. The raisins are—golden. The store where the boy buys the raisins is at the corner, down the street, he has to walk there (although it would be as well to be instantaneously transported). The store is dark. The street. Down. The corner at the end. The street, down the street, end of the street, piled with snow, snow piled cold and hard and higher than people, cuts in the snow for driveways, for the road, the snow blue, down to the end, end, the store at the end, the store. Sweet store. The raisins in the store, the storekeeper, white apron. The raisins weighed. The store is at the end of the street, they weigh raisins there. The raisin seller is an old—what, woman? The boy is not looking up. An old someone. A hand coming down for the pennies. The hand reaching forward to offer the little brown bag filled with raisins, reaching down. But the boy does not see the person at the end of the arm, the person in the white, white, white apron. I know the boy walked *back*, because I know the raisins got into the buns, the buns but not the *boulitchkas*, Russian brioches, and I cannot imagine that he spent the rest of his life in that corner store, in that store looking down, because here he is, somewhere else, out of the cold, having come in from the cold, now writing about it, looking down. I *know* that boy walked back, but I cannot see or feel that walking back. Of what use, then, is my knowledge? I can see and feel walking to the store to buy raisins. I can smell the raisins. The next thing I can feel is a dark brown piano and someone is playing it very near my head, too loudly, who knows what?, Brahms, Czerny, somebody. Where is that piano, in the store near the raisin bin? I don't think so. My grandmother's house, there, back there, in a room not so far from the kitchen, so that I can smell the *boulitchkas* in the hot oven while I listen to the music. I can't smell anything now. The boy can't smell anything as he hears the piano too loud. He can't smell but the buns bake. The sun sets. A train passes on the track running through the back yard. They served us porridge in bowls of solid silver on the old trains. They had thick starched white tablecloths and thick starched white napkins, and the waiters wore starched white linen jackets and always had very dark brown skin. The typewriter stank. I fell from a balcony and my father was aghast. The grass was green beneath my back. In the basement, among boxes and dust, was a typewriter decades old, decades and decades old, and it stank of age and dust and basement damp and ink, it had a ribbon on two black metal wheels, each key was a battleship. First words written: my name. Then: this. Between a span of files, shards, buried in Kansas. The boy walked down the street to buy raisins. With a silver brush my grandmother brushed her long long hair.

II.

Dreams do not make sense and they are not going anywhere and the blessing of dreaming is that dreams do not make sense and they are not going anywhere but in practice—that is, practically—this is hardly a blessing. (Practice: we can convince ourselves they make sense. We can convince ourselves they are going somewhere.) It is possible, of course, to subject dreams to the control of the rational and to make interpretations of them; and even to build an edifice upon the interpretations. Dreams may be subjected to the power of the rational, one more demonstration of power among the many, and an edifice may be built upon the products of this subjugation, and a city built up from these edifices, and channels of discourse rooted between districts in this city. Gomorrah, I would call this city. Dreams have nothing intrinsically to do with this city, and the blessing of dreaming is that dreams do not have anything to do with this city and are not going anywhere. Free in dreams.

But this is hardly what many would call a blessing.

12.

A man once said to me, "Learn to stutter." I did not understand him. He rapped his fingers on his desk. "That's the advice I have for you." I did not understand him. I was afraid. I ran away. I remember that he smiled. I see his smile. "Learn to stutter." I see his smile *now*. And *now* it is gone.

13.

I reject channels of discourse rooted between districts of the city of edifices built from rational analysis of dreams, and also the idea that one must wake to read. Reading has been corrupted and betrayed as it has been configured as an exercise of consciousness, as we have taken to measuring (and comparing) consciousness, alertness, and intelligence according to one's ability to use reading as a technique of extraction and exploitation. Text is taken as a geological material and intellectual extraction is valued as a means of exploiting its capital. Reading is really singing, and text should be explored for tone and for color, for shape, for form, the way dreams are explored by those who are dreaming them. We like to think to ourselves that when we read we have come upon a meaning, but later, when we awaken—*later, when we awaken*—we see that meaning is yet to be found. Meaning, indeed, is the substance yet to be found; that is what meaning is. We should read in half a slumber. In slumber she led me by funicular up a mountain and we drank martinis in a dark (lavish) bistro with candlelight and she looked at me and we talked about her son and we had martinis and her son was not there and we drank and we were looking down at the dark city, the city all twinkling, the dark rivers, the rivers conjoining, and we drank and it was dark and there in the conversation was her son and she looked at me and I did not understand the meaning but it was slumber. We should read in a half-slumber, so that reading itself is dreaming, and even upon the page of a book we can fall from a balcony, a balcony that is not there, our father aghast, sinking toward the ground and then rebounding upward into the thinner, thinner air.

14.

Rejecting the city of edifices made from dreams,

Gomorrah I would name this city. Dreams do not make sense and they are not going anywhere. A train passes on the track running through the back yard. I am looking at pages of an ancient encyclopedia with colored reproductions of jewel stones. We are both inside and outside our dreams. Some dreams move slowly and some dreams move quickly but all dreams move at the same speed. We dream in chains. There is a black-and-white drawing of a cross-section of a steamship. I fell from a balcony of a yellow brick building. I plummeted. The ground came up and I also plummeted and then I fell from the balcony of a building built of yellow bricks (that had no balcony) and the man who owned the building was short and smoked a cigar and was old and was not a pleasant man and spoke harshly to my father and didn't look at me. This was the westernmost of three buildings sitting side by side, or the southernmost, since in dreams there is no north, and behind it was a lumberyard and I played among the smartly stacked pallid two-by-fours with two boys I loved as brothers but cannot remember. Two boys. I cannot recollect anything of either, except a red shirt. Two boys, one red shirt, the stacked wood. My mother had brought cakes into a room with a huge oval polished redwood table and white satin walls and gleamy plates and golden forks and chattering strangers and after school in the kitchen my mother taught me how to make the letter D.

15.

Dreams are not myths. Dreams are the sea upon which myths sail. A boy walked down the street to buy raisins at the corner store and there in front of him was a sentence lying upon the pavement. He gathered it up, as it flopped and tried to slip away. What a beautiful sentence it was. He said it to himself over and over, so that he would always have it, and when he went home he said it again, and then he said it as he fell asleep and marveled at how much beauty was contained in that single sentence. A boy walked down the street to buy raisins at the corner store. What boy? What store? What raisins? Dreams are not myths, dreams are the sea upon which a myth can sail. When he dreamed, he dreamed a boy walking down the street finding a sentence on the pavement, and in his dream the boy picked up the sentence and said it aloud. Now and forever. Whose sentence was it then?

AUTHOR'S NOTE

It is my belief that some of the sentences used for composing some of the pieces contained here were lifted from other printed contexts both literary, editorial, educational, and critical; and then remodeled, rephrased, or reconfigured to suit the present purposes of a writer concerned not with exegesis or exposition but with music. Having acted solely from admiration of compositional style, the author or authors here abjure all intent to utilize the words of others to articulate the propositions here extended. The quoted statements of real people, such as may be found here, are authentic. If the language sometimes seems to mock the prose of another time or universe, I am convinced it is only—like Messaien taping exotic birds—to catch the precise quality of exquisite and alien melody.

ANNOUNCEMENT

All of this I now realize, but never realized before, came as a sort of dream, in the specific that I have no idea at all who wrote many of these pieces, collected the others, and assembled them into this . . . into this . . . into this entity. The authorial voice I both recognize—I have heard it before—and do not recognize. It is like a song that keeps passing through the head, or better, like a collection of songs, and one cannot—I cannot—but hum along, but I do not speak the language.

The suggestion was made to me some time back, and by a person of the greatest honesty, sensibility, kindness, erudition, and taste, that I ought to affix my own name to the title page, and while I am happy to confess that for ages I was anguished at the thought, and struggled with it and against it, finally I simply obeyed the command.

These had to be put in some order or else they would all have been mashed together in a kind of soup, so here they are, but there is no reason why anybody ought to feel obligation to begin at the beginning and end at the end. We each always find our own beginning anyway.

Toronto, Los Angeles, London, Brisbane, Copenhagen
June 2019

ABOUT THE AUTHOR

Murray Pomerance was born in 1946 in Hamilton, Ontario. He is the author of *Magia d'Amore* (Sun & Moon, 1999), *Savage Time* (Oberon Press, 2005), *Edith Valmaine* (Oberon Press, 2010), *Tomorrow* (Oberon Press, 2012), *The Economist* (Oberon Press, 2014), *A King of Infinite Space* (Oberon Press, 2016), and numerous books about cinema including *Cinema, If You Please: The Memory of Taste, the Taste of Memory* (Edinburgh University Press, 2018), *A Dream of Hitchcock* (SUNY Press, 2019), and *Virtuoso: Film Performance and the Actor's Magic* (Bloomsbury, 2019).

CPSIA information can be obtained
at www.ICGtesting.com
Printed in the USA
JSHW010544060620
6080JS00011B/76